Lost

in

Love

The Lost & Found Series

Kristen Casey

www.GallantFoxPress.com

ISBN-13: 978-0-9983914-9-6

Cover Design ©2017, 2021 Tugboat Design

Author Photo ©2016 Kathleen Oristian Photography

GALLANT FOX
PRESS

The Lost & Found Series

About this Book

If you read *Finding Love*, then you know…some characters are unforgettable.

George Hughes never minded being the spare heir—at least, he didn't mind until his brother and father almost got themselves killed six months ago. He might be brawny and good at fixing things, but without his older brother's charm or cleverness, what good is he? Then George meets a woman whose problems he can actually fix, and he knows he can't just walk away. Not when she might hold the key to his brother's recovery, and especially not when she looks and acts like his dream come true. As luck would have it, George seems to be exactly the right man for *this* job.

Poppy Whitlock can usually take care of herself, but these days she's got problems on top of problems: a less-than considerate roommate, a petty faculty advisor determined to sink her career hopes, and a looming health issue making everything else feel perilous. But then a gorgeous British man with a knack for saving the day barrels into her life, offering not only his help, but his heart—and going it alone doesn't look nearly as inviting. When Poppy saddled him with the nickname *Burning Love*, she never could have guessed how accurate it would turn out to be.

If you loved *Finding Love*, then you know…you just have to learn what happens when George and Poppy get **Lost in Love**.

Includes the bonus short story **Lucky in Love!**

Two men, two bars, and one very big secret—Charlie Hughes is about to find his perfect match, and it's going to change everything.

Chapter One

CALL IT AN occupational hazard, but Poppy Whitlock had a teensy problem with nicknames. She just could *not* help doling them out. Working in a coffee shop on a college campus would do that to a girl, she supposed. The customers might or might not give Poppy their real names, and she might or might not decide to use them. But if people were memorable enough, or maybe just came into the café often enough, sooner or later Poppy christened them with some appropriate nickname or another. Or *inappropriate*, as the case may be. It was the same in her classes. Nearly every piece of artwork that depicted a human being (and even some that didn't) ended up with a Poppy-ism. People on the T, people on the street...when she considered it, no one and no thing was really safe from her naming habit.

Given this propensity of hers, it was no great surprise, then, when a thick, muscular arm spun her around on the dance floor and her brain sputtered out, *Who's this hunk of burning love?* Once she took the guy's measure, the moniker may as well have been carved in stone. *Burning Love*, indeed. The look in his eye was enough to singe off her eyebrows. The bigger surprise, however, was that she sort of knew him. Well, in a manner of speaking. Poppy had spotted this intense hulk of a man across the bar only moments before, sitting next to two of her favorite regulars from Jazz & Java, and based on his face, he had to be a relation of the dude's.

In Poppy's world—grad student and teaching assistant by day, coffee shop manager by night—she didn't exactly get the chance to interact with many of the people she supposedly "knew." It was a quandary. She was too busy for actual friends, and she had a weird window-shopping kind of relationship with her customers, especially the regulars. She made up names for them, and truthfully, she made up lives for them, too. And Burning Love's two buddies over there just happened to be one of Poppy's only true success stories, where real life actually mirrored her own mental fiction. She'd fixed them up in her head, and then they'd fallen for each other for real. Something had happened between those two, she knew, some kind of trouble in paradise. But here they were, together again, even if they seemed a bit more awkward than they had in the past. She'd known they would hook back up eventually. They'd been too crazy in love not to.

And here, up close and personal, was their friend and probable relative. Poppy had to hand it to him—for a guy that was built like he was (namely, like a freaking house), BL had some *moves*.

"Hey, sweetheart. Mind if I join you?" he yelled.

"Why not?" she asked, all unconcerned sass. But Poppy was just dying to know what this could possibly be about. When she'd decided to blow off some steam tonight, meet up with her roommate and his boys and pretend she didn't have a ton of shit to do, she hadn't anticipated *this*.

"So, my friend says she knows you," he explained, leaning in to be heard and giving her a delectable whiff of his cologne. He pointed across the bar to the table he'd just vacated, where the café lovebirds were looking gob-smacked to see her, to say the least. And sort of like they barely knew each other, which was pretty odd. Must've been one hell of a fight.

"Um, yeah, I kind of know both of them," she admitted.

"What?" he yelled, brow wrinkling. He was doing fine dancing, but trying to dance *and* have a conversation in all this racket was clearly going to be a challenge. The band playing McGillicuddy's tonight seemed to be approximating Irish rock, but truly, they were all over the map. And not shy about the fact.

"I said, *I kind of know both of them*," Poppy tried again. She looked back and forth from him to the table. "Hey, are you two related, or what?"

He shook his head, clearly not having picked up on what she said. In exasperation, Poppy looked around the place and spotted a corner that seemed slightly more empty and quiet. She pointed it out, then grabbed his hand and towed him with her. His very large, very warm paw engulfed hers. Burning Love was totally on board—he didn't resist in the least.

Once they reached the corner, she realized it was a much smaller space than she'd anticipated, what with him crowding his bulk up in there with her. Poppy gave him another once-over. He wasn't dressed like a lot of the other club-goers. Not bad, just…not flashy. Which was a point in his favor, come to think of it.

"Now, what were you saying?" he asked, leaning a shoulder against the wall, and dropping his head down toward her.

"I just thought maybe you and that guy looked alike. Are you two related?"

He looked taken aback, but he nodded. "Yeah. He's my brother," he explained.

Poppy nodded too, and then they just stood there. Burning Love seemed to be at a loss about what to do next, and Poppy wasn't nearly tipsy enough to give him any pointers. Finally, he cleared his throat.

He rattled off something incomprehensible, his words obscured by a particularly loud guitar flourish from the stage, then grinned.

"I'm sorry?" Poppy yelled, wincing.

"So do you come here often?" he enunciated carefully, then shook his head in disgust. "It sounded much cheekier when I didn't have to scream it twice."

Poppy laughed. "What's your name?" she nearly screeched, going up on her toes to put her mouth closer to his ear. His arm slipped around her waist way too easily, helping her keep her balance. He seemed reluctant to release her, once she was flat on her feet again.

"George," he told her, sticking out his hand formally. She took it and shook, but then Burning Love didn't let go. He used the connection to pull her closer to him. "And you?"

"I'm Poppy," she called out, fully expecting to have to explain further. It wasn't the most common name in the universe, and to this day she had no idea how or why her fairly sedate parents had picked it.

But instead of being perplexed, BL just smiled at her. "Like the flower," he agreed, stealing her usual explanation. His palm stole around her waist again, then spread across her lower back, licking heat across her skin. Poppy blinked. Sure, she didn't get out that much, but the way she was reacting to this guy—it was as if she'd never run across a red-blooded male before.

George gazed at her for a long moment, then glanced around the bar again. He seemed hesitant, but then he leaned down to her.

"Hey, you want to go outside for a little bit so we can talk?" he asked her. His lips were warm, and brushed faintly against the shell of her ear. Poppy shivered.

She pulled back and thought about that. She'd checked in with her roommate Furby and his buddies when she'd first gotten there, then left them entrenched at the bar, doing shots. They'd never miss her. And just outside McGillicuddy's was the busy area of Quincy Market, lined with shops and other bars and restaurants. If she stayed close to the entrance, she would be reasonably safe. Besides, BL wasn't giving her any hinky vibes. Poppy usually got feelings about people, and George here wasn't raising a single red flag.

"Sure," she told him. "C'mon." She turned and headed for one of the glass side doors, leading right out into the market area.

Looking around, Poppy was heartened by the amount of activity out there. It wasn't loud, but it wasn't desolate, either. She'd be fine with this guy.

"Did you want to walk around a bit? Or..." she trailed off, looking at BL for guidance.

He indicated an empty bench, just a little way down the side of the building. "Why don't we cop a squat over there for a while. Sound good?"

"Sure," she agreed.

Once they had arranged themselves to face each other, he cleared his throat. Burning Love seemed to be thinking hard about what to say. It was oddly endearing that he cared enough to want to get it right.

"So—Meg in there said you work someplace called Jazz & Java?" he began.

"Yeah, I help manage it. It's a little café up on Commonwealth Avenue, near BU Central," she explained. "Like, a coffee shop with a jazzy theme."

He nodded, and Poppy had the impression he was committing that tidbit of info to memory. "Do you go to school around here?" he asked. "Or—maybe you're done already?"

"No, I'm not done yet. I'm working on my master's at BU. I'll be done next year."

"I see," George said, his eyes roving over her face and hair. Poppy fought the urge to check her hairclip, maybe wipe at the eyeliner under her eyes. 'Cause that would be *so* flipping obvious. "What do you study?" he asked.

"Museum Studies," she told him, watching for his reaction. Sometimes artsy stuff gave guys hives. Like her dad, for example. Or her ex-boyfriend Scooter. BL, however, seemed unperturbed.

"Hey, that's pretty cool," he chimed in. "My mum is into that sort of thing, too. Works with the board of the Fitzwilliam." He hesitated, then tried to explain, "Sorry. That's a museum in Britain."

"In Cambridge," she agreed. "Yeah, I know." Of course she knew. They had a Rubens. A Degas. Even a da Vinci and a Titian. And if his mother worked on the board, she was definitely not some nobody. "So…" Poppy stalled, thinking. "What do *you* do?"

George tapped his hand on the back of the bench, cracked a couple knuckles with his thumb. "I'm a contractor," he told her. He looked as if he was about to say more, but changed his mind and clammed up. It wasn't that he seemed like he was lying, exactly, but Poppy got the feeling that wasn't the whole story. Even so, there was something more interesting happening here.

"Are you British?" she asked.

"Yeah," he chuckled. "That obvious?"

"Little bit," she admitted. Your average local blue-collar dude would probably be wearing some Red Sox gear right now. Would've carried his Sam Adams outside with him, too, law be damned. "What brought you to the US?" she prodded.

"Ah, well," he hedged. "Our dad got a job at Harvard, and my younger brothers ended up in schools here. Seemed only fitting that the rest of us tag along," he told her. Again, Poppy got the idea that she was only getting half the story.

"What does your dad do there?" she prodded.

"He was guest lecturer," BL replied. He didn't elaborate—not even on his use of the past tense—and didn't look like he wanted to.

Poppy studied him. He wasn't the chattiest guy on earth, that was for sure. But he was gorgeous and strong, steady and calm and collected. He was utterly comfortable in his own skin, and didn't appear to see the need to put on a whole show to impress her. She was half in love with him already, it was so darn refreshing.

George smiled at her, a slightly sheepish, lopsided thing that made her heart take an ungainly, out-of-rhythm *thump*.

"Sorry, sweetheart," he murmured. "I'm not the best at small talk."

"At least you admit it," she grinned back. "It's the ones who think they're great at it that you really have to watch out for."

He chuckled. "That's the truth, isn't it?"

Poppy cast around for something else to say. "Hey, so...what happened with your brother and that chick he's with? I used to see them a lot, and then they sort of dropped off the face of the earth." Truth be told, they weren't exactly in there looking like they had patched things up all the way, either, Poppy thought, but she left that part alone for the time being. In fact, she'd seen the girl only a week or so ago, pushing a baby stroller and looking like her favorite puppy had died. Sizing up the man in front of her, Poppy decided to omit that juicy detail, too. For all she knew, the kid was a dirty little secret. Or even the cause of the rift itself.

George went stiff. She'd hit a nerve, she could tell.

He took a deep breath. "Well, it's kind of a long story, you know? He had an accident and can't remember some stuff from around that time. Like...Meg." George cleared his throat, seeming to need a minute to collect himself. Then he said, "I was thinking maybe we could, ah, get together one of these days. I could fill you in, maybe see if you had any ideas for how I can help get them sorted out."

Poppy stared at him. Somehow she'd read this guy all wrong. Here she'd been thinking she was being hit on by God's gift to tool belts, and he was just looking for relationship advice. For a *friend*.

BL quickly caught on to the fact that he'd made a misstep. "That's not the only reason," he rushed to add. "I'd really like to get to know you for myself, too." He shrugged, winced like it pained him every time words exited his mouth. Flicking his eyes over her face again, he finished with one awkward gesture, encompassing all that was Poppy. "I really like your...hair," BL commented weakly.

Jesus. She wanted to laugh. He was utterly awful at this, but Poppy, for some inexplicable, absurd reason, found George to be one hundred percent *adorable*. She wanted to kiss that discomfort right off his cute British face. She sighed, shaking her head at her own foolishness. This could not possibly be a good idea.

"Dude, give me your phone," she told him. "I'll put my number in there."

George, bless his heart, looked incredulous, but also totally relieved.

"Brilliant!" he exclaimed, all cheerful now. He fished it out of his pocket, called up the contact screen for her, and handed it over. The durable rubber of his case was still warm from his body, and she fought the urge to clutch it close. Poppy tapped out her name and number, handed it back, then passed her own cell phone over to him.

"Will you give me yours, too?"

His grin was sexier this time. "You got it, sweetheart," he told her. Poppy faltered. This guy was going to be *truh-bull* with a capital T if he kept that up.

Right on cue, her roommate Furby and his buddies spilled out of the side door and wandered over when they spotted her.

"Hey, Pop-Tart," he grinned, swaggering up to them like some kind of misplaced cowboy.

She introduced him to George with a grimace, "My roommate, Nate." He had become "Furby" to her soon after she'd answered his ad for a roommate, due to his excessive hairiness—long hair, furry arms, furry legs, furry face. *Furby.* He was working on his second master's degree, this one in music theory. Poppy thought his first master's, as well as his undergraduate degree, might have been in philosophy. She had zero idea what kind of job that qualified him for, and she kind of doubted he did either. Apparently, his parents were still supporting him, for the moment.

George stood up and politely extended his hand. "George Hughes."

Furby was very drunk and giggled at that. "Nathan Philby," he responded with exaggerated seriousness. His friends roared with laughter, finding that hilarious.

Poppy let out a heavy sigh, resigned to the fact that she was going to have to leave BL now and herd these imbeciles to the T. And one of them, even to her own home. She didn't want to go yet, not when things had just gotten interesting, but the fact was, she shouldn't have come in the first place. She had cancelled her teaching assistant session this evening in order to be here—not that anyone ever showed up to the night ones anyway. But she did still have to prepare her notes for next week's lecture.

Professor Stephen Cooper, a.k.a. "Mini", was brilliant and accomplished, but he could also be temperamental and erratic with his T.A.s. When she'd drawn him as a faculty advisor, she'd been ecstatic—his research work on Etruscan artifacts was a perfect complement to her thesis work. But Poppy learned early on that, among other things, he almost never used the textbook in his lectures, a fact that drove his freshman students into heart failure. He was also nothing like her considerate, nurturing professors back in Orlando. If he was going to be her advisor, he clearly expected her to be his subservient lackey. She had to know his material for the art conservation lectures better than he did, because eighteen-year-olds were insects beneath his notice. If those kids had a prayer of passing his class, Poppy had to be the one to nurse them along and hold their hands. And that meant going home now, pulling out the textbook and Mini's purported lecture notes, and trying to anticipate what he might say in class next week.

She turned to George, taking him by his hard, thick bicep, and leading him off to the side.

"I've got to get going," she sighed. "Sorry we couldn't hang out more."

George jerked his chin in Furby's direction, looking faintly pissed. "You got something going with him?"

"Furby?" Poppy laughed, incredulous. "God, no." She looked over at her roommate, who was taking a video of his friend urinating against the side of McGillicuddy's, and none too discreetly. "He's a hot mess," she added emphatically.

George looked like he agreed. "When can I see you again?" he asked.

Poppy hedged. "I'm not sure, dude," she admitted. "I'm really busy this week. Actually...I'm freaking busy all the time." As flirting went, it wasn't her best work.

"Is that a vague way of telling me you don't want to?" he pressed, eyeing her suspiciously.

Poppy grinned, liking his forthrightness immensely. No games with BL, it seemed. It was awesome. "No, I swear. I really do have a ton to do, with work and class and everything. But I'll call you tomorrow and we'll figure something out, okay? I'm sure I can fit you in *somewhere*."

"Oh, gee, thanks," he drawled, rolling his eyes.

"You're very welcome," she said, saccharine sweet and grinning.

George shook his head, smiling reluctantly at her. Next thing Poppy knew, he had her by the arms, hauling her close and dropping a hot kiss right on her lips. Once the surprise wore off, she went soft against him, sliding her palms up his strong, broad chest. George took that as an invitation, and rightly so—he opened his mouth and then, like a shock to her system, he was tasting her. BL was controlled. Sexy, possessive. And very, very good at what he was doing.

A shrieking wolf-whistle pierced the air, and Poppy jumped in his arms. George reacted too, pulling away in an instant, scanning the area for threats and shielding her against his body. They noticed Furby and friends pointing and laughing at the same moment.

Poppy clenched her teeth. That pain in the ass had just wrecked the best kiss of her life.

"Well, I guess that's that, right?" George murmured, looking back down at her.

"Yeah," she agreed. "I'll catch you later, BL." Poppy stepped out of his arms and gave him a jaunty little salute.

"See you tomorrow, then," he affirmed. Poppy frowned. Had she specified that?

She shuffled reluctantly toward the guys, steeling herself to endure their teasing and stupidity for the next half an hour or so. But when she glanced over her shoulder, George was still standing there like an enormous, sexy boulder watching her go, his brow creased in a perplexed little scowl. Meeting him—*kissing* him—was worth the headache. Worth having to play catch up with her anxious freshman charges, and worth babysitting a herd of overgrown cavemen. Poppy smiled. She'd bet her last dime that the next time she laid eyes on George Hughes, he was going to make her tell him what "BL" stood for.

Chapter Two

WHEN GEORGE SPOTTED the pinup girl of his fondest fantasies across that cheesy bar, he had no idea what his pickup line was going to be. All he knew was that he had to get to her, right that second, and stake his claim. He didn't give two shits if she was meeting someone or was there with friends. That bird was going to be his. She worked someplace called Jazz & Java, Meg said, a convenient and unexpected point of connection. It wasn't much, but George found a way to work with it. For God's sake, the rest of the room may as well have been painted in shades of gray, as vibrant and colorful as she seemed. He was *transfixed*. He'd forgotten, instantly, why he was even there.

There had been a jolt of electricity up his arm when he grabbed her. Once she levelled her direct gaze on him and started talking, wild horses couldn't have dragged him away. It was a bit of a sticky wicket. Because his goal had to be getting his brother better, *not* lining up his next bit of fluff. George had never felt much pressure being second in line for the title—his father and older brother had always been too healthy and full of life to cause him much concern over that. But after the accident last winter, he'd seen his life flash before his eyes. And there was never a man more unsuited to being a viscount, much less a bloody *earl*, than he was. He was just fine staying the honorable Mr. Hughes, thank you very much.

Besides, George knew he couldn't possibly be Poppy's type. She might have responded very nicely when he'd planted one on her at the end of the night, but girls did that sometimes, when they were out on the town. God only knew what had possessed him. In all likelihood, she'd get a look at him in the cold light of day and realize he was good for a lark and nothing more. But maybe, if he could get his foot in the door as her friend, he could get to know her in a casual, stealthy, wouldn't-see-him-coming kind of way. Perhaps that wasn't the best metaphor. As George had moved against her on the crowded dance floor last night, he knew he wanted her to see him coming in the worst possible way. And Lord, did he want to see her do the same. No question. He had just needed to think fast, figure out a way to work the angle, and eventually their blistering chemistry would have to make her see reason. Just like that, George had known what he was going to do. He could tell himself that he was helping Edward, and he could get to know the lovely Poppy at the same time. As plans went, it had seemed foolproof.

George paced back and forth across his living room, trying to ignore his younger brother Charlie's amused gaze. There was just one problem. Poppy had said she would call him, and she Wasn't. Fucking. Calling. He checked his cellphone. It was ten o'clock in the morning. If she was really planning on fitting him in today like she'd implied, shouldn't she have rung him up by now? He had crap he needed to get done today, too. She wasn't the only busy one. But somehow the thought of missing her text or call had him paralyzed at home, wearing a veritable canyon into his apartment carpet.

"Well, you know what they say, right?" Charlie piped up. Damn it. George was so bloody distracted, he kept forgetting his little brother was there. *Why* was the twat there? Didn't they feed the cheeky bastard at his university?

"No, Charles," George replied absently. He'd been checking and rechecking his phone all morning to see if there was a text from her. He'd been careful, though. Charlie probably hadn't noticed. "What do they say?"

"Find a Poppy, pick her up, then all day you'll have good luck," Charlie sang.

"Seriously, that's just rubbish," George grumbled, glaring at him.

"No, it's not. I saw it in a film once," his brother retorted. As if that was a perfectly reasonable thing to say.

George stalked over and slugged Charlie in the arm. It seemed like the soundest course of action. "Anyway, I didn't pick her up," he muttered.

"Maybe not, but if you really fancy her, it's only a matter of time," Charlie asserted.

"What's that supposed to mean?" George demanded. He didn't much care for his brother's tone.

"That in the next week or two, I fully expect you to sling her over your shoulder, stomp off, and stash her away in your cave," Charlie replied airily.

George threw his hands up in utter exasperation. "What have I ever done, actually in your presence, to make you think of me like that?" It was maddening, really.

"Uh, acted like a caveman," Charlie said, as if he had a screw loose just for asking.

George glared at Charlie, who merely grinned smugly back at him. He paced away across the room, checked his phone, then turned and came back toward Charlie. This, apparently, was going to be his life now—stuck between Edward and Charlie forevermore, in the eternal mad roster of brothers. One irreverent goofball on the left hand (two if you counted Fred, and he'd never shut his mouth if you left *him* out), and one irreparably damaged shell of a man on the right.

But no. He refused to believe that of Edward. George owed it to his steadfast, dutiful big brother to find a fix for this temporarily tricky situation they were in. God knew Edward had smoothed over plenty of their messes in his day. While George might not have Edward's way with words, or his finesse with people, he damn well knew how to fix shit. He was going to find a solution to this problem if it killed him. And it might.

George had been keeping their business and their family going almost single-handedly for months now. He was really fucking *tired*. Tired of nursing Edward along, dropping carefully worded hints that might help him recover his memory without pissing him off. Tired of shepherding his two little brothers—making sure they got where they were supposed to go, and did what they were supposed to do. Tired of nurturing his mother and worrying over his father. Tired of trying to fill Ed's shoes at their company, when everyone knew it wasn't one of his strengths.

George could build things. Repair things. Restore an old pine floor or some antique crown molding. He could lord it over a crew of electricians and carpenters like a *boss*. But pulling in new business and sweet-talking clients? That was Edward's purview. George wanted his brother back, doing all the things he did best, because shit was going to fall apart in the worst way if George had to be the one keeping it afloat much longer. Also, George just plain missed his brother. The guy walking around in Edward's skin right now was a total dick. What a bloody nightmare.

Charlie clapped him on the back a little harder than was strictly necessary, jolting George from his rumination.

"So? What was she like, anyway?" he prodded. "I have to say, Georgie, she didn't seem to be your usual type."

What the hell was this nonsense? He didn't have a type. "I don't have a—"

"Five foot ten, about nine stone with curves, straight brunette hair, throaty laugh, dimples optional..." Charlie interjected.

"Fuck," George grouched. Nailed it right on the head, the little blighter. Besides, dimples weren't even kind of optional. His brother laughed, as if reading George's thoughts to the letter.

He clutched his cell phone in his hand, and smoothed the screen up and down his thigh, the thick protective case dragging against his worn jeans. He didn't bother with a ringer—it was usually too loud where he was working to hear it anyway. But it would vibrate if Poppy called or texted, and then he wouldn't have to keep checking to see if he'd missed something from her. Because his irritating little brother was almost certain to notice *that*.

Yeah.

"Hasn't rung you up yet, has she?" Charlie inquired, a bit smugly, if you asked him.

George took a deep, fortifying breath. Mainly in lieu of decking Charles right in the face, which Mum would almost certainly frown upon. But also because he was about to tell Charlie the truth, and that could only lead to torment.

"No. She hasn't."

"Must have been disappointed, poor thing," his brother commented, examining his cuticles.

"I assure you, she was not," George huffed. He sounded stiff, even to his own ears.

"Ah. So you *did* sleep with her?" Charlie gloated.

George wheeled on him. "Christ, Charles. Give it a rest, would you?" He supposed he ought to take it as a compliment to his sexual prowess and his powers of persuasion, but they'd been in a packed bar. And then, outside in a crowded tourist area lined with shops and restaurants. Where, exactly, was George supposed to have nailed her?

"All right. I will. If *you* call *her*," Charlie countered.

"If I ..." George stuttered, coming to a halt in the middle of the room.

"... call *her*. Yes," Charlie confirmed.

George scowled. In all his twenty-five years, he'd never hurt for female company. But he was more of a one-date bloke. He certainly could manage a nice text the next morning, especially if he'd bagged the woman—that was just the gentlemanly thing to do. *Calling* a girl, however, implied a certain interest in seeing her again, and George had never been much interested in repeat performances. Once the itch was scratched, it tended to stay that way.

The problem with Poppy, as he saw it, was twofold: A) He *hadn't* actually slept with her last night, though he bloody well wanted to. And B) He could *not* stop thinking about her. About her cherry-red painted lips, or about slipping those cute little glasses off her face, certainly. But also about what she did with her days, and what made a woman like her tick. With a sickening churn of his stomach, George realized that none of that had a single thing to do with Ed, or how Miss Poppy could help him fix his brother. And that was the worst news yet, because it meant that for the first time, George himself was at risk.

"It's okay, you know," Charlie commented.

"I know that," George groused.

"Do you?" his brother asked. "Because for some reason, I suspect you think you're being disloyal to Edward by asking this girl out."

"That's stupid," George muttered. Even if it was true.

"You're right, George, it *is* stupid," Charlie agreed. "You do realize that no one expects you to stop living while Edward works this thing out for himself? It wasn't your fault it happened, and it's not your responsibility to fix it."

Oh, but it was. It *was*. Charlie had no bloody idea. George could not waste even a moment that could be better spent helping Edward to remember.

"*Call her*," Charlie urged. "Please, George. You deserve to be happy."

George snorted.

"Okay, fine. You deserve to be content," Charlie amended, all snark.

George wasn't going to sit here arguing the toss with his ridiculous brother all morning. He wheeled away and headed toward his bedroom, his decision made. Poppy had said she was busy all the time, so clearly she'd gotten diverted and forgotten to call him. But George needed to meet with her, and find out if she knew anything at all that could help him get Edward to remember last autumn. And he wasn't the sort of man to sit around waiting for something he wanted. If it was important to him, like this was, George went out and got what he needed. He sat heavily on the side of his mattress, scrolled through his contacts, and found her name. Before he could change his mind, he called her up.

When Poppy answered, she was out of breath. Of course she was. Busy, just like she'd said.

"George?" she asked, skipping preliminaries.

"Hi, sweetheart," he said, clutching the phone. "How's it going?"

"Good!" she chirped. George heard a door slam in the background, and wondered where she was.

"I thought we might try to meet up today," he told her. "Maybe grab some lunch." He held his breath, straining to hear how she took that.

She groaned. "Oh, man, I'm sorry BL," she told him. "I am totally swamped today. I don't think I have time for lunch."

George frowned. There was that nickname again—*BL*. What could that possibly mean?

"All right. Coffee, then. You can show me where you work," he persisted.

Poppy went silent for a long minute, and George thought he'd wrecked things, pushed her too hard. He hated how that felt, the disappointment curdling his gut.

But then she said, "Listen, will you be around the BU campus around one? I have some time between classes—we could meet up for a little bit then if you wanted?"

Hope bloomed. "Yeah, sure, I could do that," George agreed. He would've met her in Timbuktu if that's what she wanted, but BU worked, too. "Where should I meet you?"

"How about Marsh Plaza?" she asked. "That's right on my way to my next class."

"Done. See you then," he told her. Now he was hearing traffic noise in the background. Miss Poppy was on the move.

"Yup. Bye," she said, and the line went dead.

George sat there a moment longer, clutching his phone and picturing her glossy black hair with its vivid blue streaks, and fighting back a wave of guilt. He had to keep reminding himself that this was about Ed, not about him. But as he thought back over the night before, he remembered something. After Poppy had left with her asinine flatmate and his friends, George had wandered back into McGillicuddy's. And there, gyrating on the dance floor like nothing at all was amiss, had been Edward and Meg. One would never have guessed, to look at them, what they had been through in the last six months. It had made George feel a little better about cutting out on them for a bit to talk to Poppy, and he clung to the image now. It was going to be all right. He'd find some way to fix it so that Meg didn't give up on him before Ed got better, and George didn't have to give up Poppy in the process. With a renewed sense of determination, he stood and headed back out to the living room. First things first. If George was going to make any progress at all today, Charlie needed to get the hell back to campus, and out of his hair.

Chapter Three

POPPY FUSSED WITH her hair in the bathroom mirror, twisting it up at the back of her head and then brushing it down again. This week it was black with electric blue streaks. It was close to what she wanted, but it was still bugging her. It wasn't *quite* what she was in the mood for. The blue was only semi-permanent—maybe she'd strip it out, try something warmer. No, she thought, her mind circling back to the big brute from last night. Something *hotter.* Yep. That ought to do it. Just then, her phone rang. Sadly, it was not BL.

"Hey, Daddy-O," she answered, seeing her parents' number on the screen. She didn't have to guess which one it would be—they were like clockwork. Her father placed the call, then got all the family business (according to him, anyway) taken care of. Then her mom took over, smoothing ruffled feathers, cajoling Poppy, and otherwise setting the family ship to rights. Very, very predictable. Poppy could almost even guess why they were calling.

"Hi, Kiddo. How's it going?" She was twenty-four years old, and still *Kiddo* to him. No wonder she had a thing about nicknames.

"I'm good. What's new down there?"

"Well, Nicole finally quit. I just thought you should know, in case you wanted her spot." The "spot" in question being, of course,

Nicole's customer service job at the Whitlock Auto Parts store, where Poppy had last worked as a high school student. And where she had vowed never to work again.

"Dad, seriously," she muttered.

"I'm perfectly serious."

"I *know*. That's the problem. I'm in school. I have a job. Two jobs, if you count the teaching assistant thing. And I'm trying to land an amazing internship for this summer! Why would you ask me to take a job in your store, in *Orlando*?"

"Technically, it's Altamonte Springs," he grumbled.

"*Dad!*"

"Well, it sure as hell pays better than that artsy-fartsy stuff," he huffed.

"It pays minimum wage! And I happen to love art. I've *always* loved art. What the heck do I know about cars?" Poppy screeched.

"Well, you sure seemed to like talking about cars with that nice young man you dated from the garage while you were still here. He was a gearhead, and you liked him just fine."

Poppy groaned. That kid had been adorable—lean and tattooed, black pomaded hair and sparkling blue eyes. To her rockabilly soul, he'd been as good as young Elvis.

"Daddy, I was eighteen. It was years ago!" And that kid could've been talking about socks and Poppy would've hung on his every word. "Besides, Scooter is like…a *chiropractor* right now." In Georgia. With a wife and a kid, not necessarily acquired in the traditional order.

"So? There's good money in that, or so your mother tells me."

"Can we focus?" Poppy begged, feeling the conversation, and her composure, spiraling.

"All I'm saying is, if you wanted to pack it in and come home, there's a place for you here," her dad said defensively.

"I get that. And thank you. But I'm gonna stick it out here a while longer," she retorted.

"If you insist. But, Popsy?" *Shit.* If he was calling her "Popsy", she was going to hate the next part.

"Yeah?" she asked warily.

There was a click and some shuffling, the blessed sound of her mother finally picking up the other line. And none too soon, if you asked Poppy.

"So help me God, Josh, don't you even *think* about telling Poppy she's not getting any younger," her mom snapped.

"Margaret, I did no such thing."

"Yet. But you were about to," she intoned knowingly.

"Guys? Could we stop? Please?" Poppy begged.

"Joshua, hang up," her mother ordered.

"All right, already. Bye, Pops. Come home and see us sometime soon."

"I will, Dad. Bye."

Her father's extension clicked and her mother snorted in exasperation.

"He told you about Nicole?" her mom confirmed, never one to beat around the bush.

"Yup," Poppy grumbled.

Annnnd it was off to the races. "That little hussy had *another* fling at work. This time with th new guy, Mike, from the tire shop? It totally set off Nick and Vinny again, not that she should've stuck around with Vinny. Anyway, your father got sick of having to break up the fights."

"Mom, you need a hobby, man," Poppy told her, wincing.

"I do just fine. How are *you* doing?" she countered pointedly.

"Oh, you know. The usual," Poppy hedged.

"So…working too much, eating scraps on the fly, barely sleeping, and…what? Fussing with your hair color every other week?" her mother inquired archly.

Bingo. A direct hit. "Pretty much," Poppy agreed.

"You are aware that at some point, something's got to give, right? You're burning yourself out, Penelope Helen," Margaret scolded.

"Mom, I'm fine." But of course, the use of her full name signaled that things were anything but fine.

"I would like very much to believe you."

Poppy just sighed. What could she possibly say to that? Instead, she rubbed at her chest, which was feeling uncomfortably tight.

Her mother's sigh was even bigger. "All right. Well…have you met anyone?"

Poppy *had*. And while she didn't have a ton to share, she could at least give her mother this.

"Actually, yeah. I did," she admitted.

There was a stunned pause. *Gotcha there, Mamacita*, Poppy thought.

"Really."

"Yup. His name is George, and he's British," Poppy told her.

And smokin' hot, but better to leave that part out. Poppy could almost *hear* her mother's eyes blinking furiously as she tried to process that information.

"Is he—does he…did you meet him at school?" she finally stuttered out.

Huh. Well, this was where it started to fall apart, she supposed.

"Um, no. In a bar," Poppy confessed.

"What does he do?" her mother demanded.

"Not sure yet," she hedged blithely. George had said he was a contractor, but that could mean any number of things. Contract killer? Not mom-approved. Contract attorney? Workable.

"Oh. Well. Okay, it's good that you're getting out some. Just be careful."

"I always am."

"I know, honey." Her mom's voice softened.

"Margie?" her father's voice cut in abruptly, too loud and startling on the other extension.

"Yes?"

"Do you know where the bologna is?"

Poppy rolled her eyes. Never failed. And who even ate bologna anymore, anyway?

"Josh, you finished that yesterday."

"Oh. Right. Sorry. Bye again, Pops."

"Bye, Dad."

He clicked off, and Poppy waited for what she knew was coming.

"Poppy, honey, I'd better go make that helpless man some damn lunch before he takes apart my whole kitchen."

And there it was. The final sign off in another typical Whitlock family convo.

"Roger that, Mom. Talk to you soon."

"Love you," her mom called, then hung up.

"Love you, too," Poppy said to the empty air.

Poppy gave up on her hair, twisting it up into a hasty chignon on the back of her head and tying on a scarf as a headband. She was just tying the laces of her Doc Martens when her cell phone went off. Scrambling for her bag, she fished it out, and this time it *was* George.

"George?" she squeaked, hoping she didn't sound too eager, but guessing she probably did.

"Hi, sweetheart," his deep, sexy voice said.

Poppy had to think fast. In a rush, she remembered *sort of* insinuating she would see him sometime today. She'd already gotten an agitated text from Missy, one of the baristas at Jazz, asking her to cover her shift this evening. And her conversation with her folks hadn't exactly left her enough time to get to her teaching assistant session on time this morning, not if she swung by Mini's office like she'd planned. Oh well, the freshmen could cool their heels for a few minutes. She had to see Professor Cooper. Ms. Sargent-Chaffee had left yet another voice mail for Poppy the day before, reminding her that Mini's recommendation was still missing from her internship application. She looked at her kitchen clock frenetically. Her own curation class wasn't until two. If her TA session didn't run long, she could probably see George for a few minutes after that. With that settled, she gave George the deets, grabbed all her stuff, and booked it for campus.

Her visit with Mini took less time than she anticipated, considering what a blowhard he could be. He didn't particularly want to talk about her thesis, the details of which were still taking shape in her mind. In a general sense, she hoped to underscore how even the most modern of artists were influenced by history's earliest creators. She knew she would profile Kiki Bartucci, a native Floridian sculptor and darling of the edgy modern art scene. Her primitive, rough-hewn works were eerily reminiscent of some of the Estrucan artifacts that Professor Cooper was researching, which was why she'd been happy to be matched with him as an advisor in the first place. Poppy *had* learned a lot from Professor Cooper about the Etruscans (especially in the last twenty minutes), but she'd learned even more about all the ways a person could be a petty, self-absorbed ass. In true form, he was even less interested in hearing about the recommendation he was supposed to write for her. Eventually, she had to give up, and make her less-than-graceful exit.

Poppy was only ten minutes late for her TA session, one floor down from Mini's office. That didn't keep her precious freshmen from feeling supremely annoyed, and they clearly wanted to torture her in return. Only five of the twelve registered students had shown up, though even that was more than usual. One of those promptly fell asleep, head pillowed on his folded arms. Out of the remaining four, one girl asked a legitimate question, then left in a great flurry of windbreaker and backpack directly after Poppy answered her. And then, the class's primary know-it-all monopolized the discussion for the next forty minutes. Professor Cooper's lectures were currently covering conservation of the Dutch masters, and Poppy had things she needed to make sure the students understood. Loudmouth Sanjit wanted to talk Taj Mahal. *At length*. It was maddening. Especially considering that she now would not have time to eat lunch and study before her own curation seminar. She hadn't done the reading for today—she'd sacked out cold last night, before she'd even gotten three paragraphs in.

Poppy wrapped things up with a reminder that their papers were due by the end of the week. Then she tore out of the building and across Comm Ave, narrowly being missed by a cyclist before setting foot on Marsh Plaza. Her cell buzzed in her pocket, the first couple bars of "Smokey Joe's Café", and she whipped it out to see what fresh hell this was.

I'm here.

Oh, shit. George. Somehow she'd completely forgotten. Poppy tried to catch her breath, as her eyes scanned the loggia to the right of the chapel. Her chest was tight, her throat was tight, and she was beginning to see stars at the edges of her vision. No. No, *not now*, this could *not* be happening now. Poppy forced her feet to move in his direction. BL's size made him easy to spot in the swirling crowd of students pouring out of the classroom building to the right, some cutting through the walkway's arches to reach the plaza and the street, others heading toward the student center behind the chapel. George was taller and broader than most of the kids, and the only person standing still where he leaned against one of the stone arches watching for her. A pair of girls rushing by knocked into Poppy, giggling out a "Sorry!" as they ran to catch the T. Poppy managed another few steps, getting truly scared now. She couldn't breathe. She was going to pass out, probably die right here in the middle of the plaza, and likely get trampled to death.

But George had found her. He raised a hand in greeting, his brow furrowed as he watched her approach. Solid, sturdy George, a grown man, standing there immovable as the kids parted around him, seemed like the only anchor she could find in a suddenly terrifying sea of people. Poppy focused everything she had on him, her unsteady steps ping-ponging her back and forth as students pushed past her. She was panicking. She had to get out of here, and fast. When she finally reached him, George took in her appearance, noting her face and her trembling and her gasping breaths. His expression turned dark, that concerned frown morphing into a ferocious scowl as he hooked a thick arm around her waist and yanked her into his personal space. His head swung around, searching, and Poppy managed to point.

"There," she wheezed, indicating the side door of the chapel.

George hustled her out of the flow of foot traffic, hauled open the heavy wood door, and had her inside the vestibule in moments. She knew how she must look—it was hard to forget this sort of thing, even though it had been years since it last happened this badly. She would be ashen and sweating soon, if she wasn't already. She sounded like she'd sprinted a mile on the way here. And she was staggering like a drunk.

"I think I'm going to be sick," Poppy told him, distressed.

George slipped her messenger bag off her shoulder, then man-handled her through the church's nave so he could tuck her into one of the back pews. On the way, he leaned down and snagged a trash can from beneath the wooden lectern holding the church bulletins, then placed it in the aisle, presumably in case she decided to actually toss her cookies in the house of God. Poppy hunched into herself, trying not to die.

George sat down next to her and studied her, from the black bandanna she'd tied around her hair and knotted at her crown, to the toes of her hot pink patent-leather combat boots. Poppy propped her feet up on the red leather kneeler, rubbed her hands up and down her legs, and looked wildly around while she continued to hyperventilate. It was quiet and dim, serene and calm, and they seemed to be mostly alone. Poppy still felt like she might bolt at any minute, though she doubted she'd get far. As meltdowns went, this one was a doozy. Everything felt very weird, very surreal, right now. Everything…except George.

"Do you need a doctor, sweetheart?" he asked quietly. "Is it…asthma maybe?"

"No!" she gasped out, horrified. "I'm fine."

He didn't seem entirely convinced of that, and who could blame him? George glanced around, apparently deciding that this was, in fact, the best place for her at the moment. And if he needed help…yup, there was a man up on the altar, peeking at them while arranging things in a small side cabinet. George gave the guy a little nod and wave to let their curious witness know he had this handled. But Poppy had no doubt the dude would stick around unobtrusively, just in case calamity struck the chapel. Her chest was still heaving, her breaths erratic and wheezing while she struggled to get in air. Her heart was hammering a mile a minute. George put a large warm hand on her back, steadying her.

"How about you try putting your head between your knees?" he suggested. Poppy was fairly sure he had no flipping idea what you were supposed to do in this situation. But it did seem like a plan, of sorts.

She nodded and doubled over, hugging her knees and hiding her face. George stroked her back, moving his palm slowly up and down, up and down, trying to calm her. After a couple minutes, she sat up again, still wheezing. He brushed a hank of hair from her cheek.

"Jesus," he whispered, then glanced at the crucifix over the altar in what appeared to be silent apology. He shook his head. "Terrific. Blaspheming in church. My mum would be so proud." Then he refocused on her. "Tell me how you're doing, love."

Poppy shook her head quickly. "Can't…talk," she rasped.

"You're sure you don't need a doctor?"

She nodded. "Think it's…panic…attack," she forced through numb lips.

"Shit," he murmured. "Okay." He looked perturbed, but determined to see her through it.

Poppy gazed back at him, trying desperately to calm down, to break out of the spiral she was in, but she just couldn't. Her eyes leapt from him, to the windows, to the altar, and back again. Always back to him.

"Right. Shall I talk then?" he asked. Oh God, his eyes—focused as intently on her as she was on him. When Poppy nodded gratefully at him, George looked like he would do anything in the world for her in that moment. She wanted to cry for what a gift that was.

George looked around at the stained glass windows and the exquisite wood ribbing soaring overhead and crisscrossing the high vaulted ceiling, while he searched for inspiration.

"You remember my brother, from last night?" he asked, finally.

Poppy nodded again, watching him. He kept stroking her back in a soothing pattern.

"He would love this place," George said. "He's an architect, like our dad. Now, Dad would probably love to rip out all the carvings in here, maybe add some kind of chrome helix-looking thing up the middle," George chuckled.

Poppy smiled as best as she could, wishing she had the breath to say what she was thinking—about that being an efficient stairway to heaven. But George kept talking, looking around.

"But not Edward. Ed would tell you the whole history of this place, what every last curlicue was called, why each grain of wood was special. And then he'd want to send me in here to restore it all, so it would stand another hundred years." George glanced at her, checking to see how Poppy was doing. Her breathing was evening out a bit, and she didn't seem to be shaking as badly. But she imagined her color was probably still God-awful. At least her eyes weren't jumping around so much. She could better focus on his serious, square-jawed face now. Poppy put a hand on his leg—her fingers looked small and pale against the strong muscles of his thigh.

"Keep going," she asked with difficulty. "Please?"

He nodded. "Edward is...God, he's so smart. Took firsts in all his classes, but not, you know...awkward, book-smart. He's always had a way with words, with people. Just a really kind, sorted person, you know? Not a wuss—I mean, the bloke was in the army, even did some boxing. Hell, he's got three little brothers, right? Ed's got a monster of a right hook."

Poppy smiled at that, trying to encourage him. On some level she understood that this was extraordinary, that this reticent man was finding a way to be chatty for her. And George kept going, forcing out word after word in what he probably assumed sounded like a horrifying stream of nonsensical blather. To her, though—to her it felt like a lifeline.

"I'm not like him," George told her. "I can't...I can't say things the way he can. I could probably show you how they cut the stones in this floor, or how they plastered the walls or carved the wood, but...yeah. I don't exactly have Ed's finesse."

Poppy squeezed his knee, trying to look sympathetic, but deciding, for the moment, to stay silent. Tentatively, George took her hand in his, and finding it freezing, pressed it between his palms to thaw it.

"More?" he asked, looking like he was hoping to God that she was sick of listening to him.

But Poppy nodded. Of course she did.

"More. Okay, let's see. Well, I told you last night what happened to Ed. He and our father were in a car accident last December, and one of the things that happened is that he's lost pretty much all of last autumn in his mind. Just...flat out can't recall it. Normally, he's sound as a pound, but now..." George ran a shaky hand over his face. "I'm trying to get him back together with Meggers. I'm hoping she will help him remember stuff. They were really brilliant together."

Poppy nodded. She'd known them, too, though obviously not as well as George had. She understood.

"Do you think...they will get back together?" she asked. She had enough breath to say that, at least.

He shook his head. "I'm working on it," he told her. She'd never seen someone look so beleaguered.

Poppy made a decision. "She came in," she told him haltingly. "To the café. She had a...a kid...in a stroller." She peered at him, trying to gauge his reaction to that.

BL blew out a huge breath. "Oh, hell. Yeah, you must have seen her the same day I did. That was her nephew, thank Christ. Just about gave me a fucking heart attack." Now he scrubbed his big hands through his close-cropped hair. Poppy wondered, watching him, what it would look like if it grew longer. Would it be the same color as his brother's? Would it be stick-straight or have some wave? It seemed really important that she know that.

"But also," George went on, giving her another once-over to ascertain if she was still breathing, "Ed and I have a business together. We restore and renovate historic properties. Edward's accident was six fucking months ago, and he's just now starting to get back into things. I've been trying to, you know...hold the proverbial baby in the family, do all the shit that needs to get done, but..." He trailed off, like he wasn't sure what else to say.

Poppy wondered how he might finish that statement. That he couldn't do it anymore? George was no whiner, and he definitely didn't strike her as a quitter. She imagined he would keep plugging away until he was dead in the ground. Still, he was in a heck of a position.

"Anyway," he said, "it's a lot—running the crews and the office at the same time. I'm trying to make sure Ed gets better, and my little brothers aren't going feral, and my parents are surviving..."

Poppy frowned, picking up on his last words. She pressed her hand to her chest, willing her heart into some kind of normal cadence, so she could participate in this conversation more. Because Burning Love over here was turning out to be *fascinating*.

Naturally, he picked up on her expression immediately, and he paused. "Oh. So, our dad was in the accident, too, right? He's having to learn to walk again. It's charming," he commented drily.

"Are they here?" Poppy asked. Her voice sounded almost normal again, so that was progress. She reached up and untied the bandanna she'd used to hold her hair back today, then blotted at her clammy forehead and cheeks, trying to be careful of her makeup. She wasn't feeling quite so cold anymore, but that was no wonder. The big man next to her generated a lot of heat.

"No, still back in the UK. Are you starting to feel a bit better, then?" he inquired. He looked desperately hopeful. The poor guy was probably praying she was, because he likely had no clue what else he could possibly say. Poppy suspected George hadn't strung this many words together in years, if ever.

"Yeah, I'm good," she told him, weary of being a victim to this stupid reaction that she could not control. Pissed that it had returned now, of all the inconvenient times. She stood up quickly, hands on the pew in front of her, then plopped back down just as abruptly, feeling green.

"*Almost*," Poppy amended sheepishly.

"Here, why don't you put your feet up for a minute? I don't think they'll mind," George said. He turned sideways and leaned his shoulder blades against the high side of the pew, pulling Poppy to lean back against his broad chest. She stretched her legs along the polished wood bench, crossing her feet at the ankles. Her bright pink boots, with their black laces tied just so, seemed wildly incongruous here. She could smell the sweet apple scent of her shampoo, but it was mixed with something else—George's own devastatingly male scent drifted around her, too. Poppy didn't like not being able to see his face, but she really, really liked being enveloped in his powerful arms.

"It's probably obvious that I'm not an architect, right?" he mused, finding more thoughts to soothe her with. "I'm the brawn of the operation, clearly. Mum had me get a business degree, but I spent all my summers and holidays working construction. I apprenticed with carpenters and tilers and masons, even learned a little electrical stuff. Some plumbing. You know. Can't tell if your crew is fucking up if you don't know what they're doing in the first place," he explained. Then, he muttered a half-hearted, "Sorry."

"For what?" she inquired.

"I've just realized that I'm dropping a shitload of f-bombs."

Poppy snorted out a startled giggle, unable to help herself. Only BL could make a panic attack in a chapel *enjoyable.*

"Among other selected curses," he grinned against her hair. They sat in silence for a minute or two.

"George?" she asked.

"Yeah?"

"Thanks for helping me," she said softly. She would be mortified by this whole interlude later, but somehow she knew that it would irritate him to no end if she mentioned it now.

"Anytime, sweetheart," he murmured. And God help her, Poppy believed him.

"I'm sorry," she said. "This had to have been really weird."

"Naw," he drawled. "This rocks."

Looking around, at the beauty that surrounded her in this quiet space, and the beauty of the rough-hewn man who held her, Poppy realized...it kind of did. Right this second was the best she'd felt in months. She took that in, then dropped her head back against his shoulder. Sweetly, he bent his own head and pressed his cheek to hers.

"Yeah, it kind of does, doesn't it?" she agreed.

"Mm-hm." He tightened his strong, thick arm just a touch around her. "So…does this happen to you a lot?" The worry in his voice was evident. Poppy's instinct, as always, was to downplay things.

"Oh," she hemmed. "No." And then, "Well…"

"Well?" he prompted.

"Yes," she admitted. "More lately. This one was…the worst I've had in a long time. It used to happen in high school, but it went away once all the family drama of me picking a school and a major died down."

"But now it's back."

"Certainly seems that way," Poppy agreed.

"Why was your major so controversial?" George asked.

"I got my undergrad in museum studies down in Florida. Now I'm getting a master's in art history here at BU, with a museum studies focus," she explained pointedly.

"What's wrong with that?" George asked, confused. "My mum does a lot with the Fitzwilliam museum at home. I told you that, right?"

"Sure," she said.

"She would have been thrilled if I'd studied something like that."

"My dad runs an auto parts store and a tire shop," Poppy explained flatly. Really, what more explanation was needed?

"Aaah," George said into her hair. Then he shifted around, so he could meet her eyes. He looked amused. "Do you know what? We've sort of traded roles," he chuckled.

"How do you figure?" Poppy asked, confused.

"You had the blue-collar parents and you went into the arts. I had the artsy parents and went into the trades. It's kind of smashing, when you think about it. Balances the cosmic scales, and all that." His eyes, a soft light brown with ridiculously long eyelashes, twinkled. Poppy blinked, trying to assimilate *that*. But then his words registered.

"I'm sorry," Poppy said. "Did you just say *cosmic scales*, dude?"

"As a matter of fact, yes, I did," he answered, droll as could be. "And now I know for sure that you're better, because you just called me *dude*."

"Very funny," Poppy snapped.

He sighed, looking satisfied and content. But they both knew this encounter was over.

"You said you had a lot on your plate today. Can I help you get anywhere?" he asked her.

Poppy glanced down at her watch, horrified by what she saw there. "Shit! No, I'm good. But I do have to get going. Like—*now*." She stood up again with much better results, then looked around for her bag.

George fished it out from under the pew, then handed it to her. "Why don't I drop you off?" he tried again.

"No, really," she insisted. "It's just across the street. It will be faster to walk."

"Fair enough," he said. "If you're sure you're okay." Then George hesitated.

"Okay, well, I'll see you around?" Poppy tried, searching for a way to say goodbye after what he'd just done for her.

"I'd like to see you again," he told her. "Ideally under different circumstances."

She laughed, because the alternative was wincing or crying, and he'd already witnessed enough dramatics from her today.

"Shall I text you? Set something up?" he tried. George's cell was buzzing in his pocket. With a look of irritation, he pulled it out, then turned aside to hold a lightning fast, murmured conversation. Once he'd ended the call, BL just looked at her, shook his head in defeat, and explained, "That was Edward."

"I'd like that," Poppy said, returning to his prior request. Though how she was going to fit him in, she had no idea. She was already late as hell for her curation seminar. If she covered Missy's shift that evening, the rest of the day was shot, and tomorrow looked no different. At some point, Poppy had to eat. And sleep.

George rose and moved out of the pew, gesturing for her to precede him down the aisle. In moments, they were out the doors, standing in the bright spring sun on the steps of the chapel. And Poppy, irrationally, suddenly did not want to let him go. On impulse, she rose up on her toes and dropped a quick kiss on his cheek. George froze, looking surprised.

"Bye," she smiled up at him.

But before she could take off, he'd grabbed her in his arms and dipped his head, planting a longer, hotter kiss smack on her lips. It wasn't quite as heady as his kiss from the night before, but it was plenty special nonetheless.

"Well, then," Poppy breathed out, once he'd released her.

George looked smug. "Bye, sweetheart," he grinned, then strolled down the stairs with a little wave and sauntered away.

Poppy's eyes darted around Marsh Plaza as she wondered who might have just witnessed that display. Even as late as she was, she still stood there and watched him go, waiting until she couldn't see his back anymore before she went down the stairs and on her way. Poppy had to admit, she was a little dumbfounded that such a burly dude could be so tender and caring. But, if that was what she had to look forward to, she was really, really hoping he'd call *soon*.

Chapter Four

FOR THE NEXT few days, George's brain kept circling back to the look on Poppy's face when he first spotted her in the plaza. True, he'd also dwelt a bit on the enticing scent that had drifted up from her slender frame to fill his lungs. And he might have spent a minute or two contemplating the way she fit so perfectly cradled in his arms. He'd have to be dead not to think about those things.

But mainly, he couldn't shake the image of her desperate, frantic expression. Hell, she looked like she'd been in the wars. And the more he Googled panic attacks on his cell phone, the worse he felt. At the pace she was driving herself, her condition was likely to only get worse. Poppy had seemed peculiarly cavalier about the whole thing—as if she intended to take the "*If I don't look at it, it will go away*" approach. George was worrying over her like his damn grandmother would, and he hated how the feeling was taking over his life.

So, on the fourth day he tried to see her again, and the third time Poppy cancelled on him, George had had enough. He knew in his bones that there was something between them. He just needed a chance to remind her. He checked his watch, realized she'd be closing up the café in about an hour, and decided to see how she was in person. Poppy was at work, after all—she would be something of a captive audience. How many people could possibly be loitering there at this hour, anyway? George could keep her company, try to assess her mental state, and then drive her home afterward. It seemed so simple, so low-key. Foolproof, really.

Except, just as he was getting ready to walk out the door, his phone rang. And not his mobile, either. It was his landline, which he mostly forgot existed, but his mum insisted he keep active. That could only mean one thing. George blew out his breath with impatience, swung back into his flat, and slammed the door. London, as they say, was calling.

Okay, not London—more like Cambridgeshire. But it was in fact his father, and after a quick mental calculation, he felt no small amount of trepidation about why the *pater familias* might be ringing up his son at nearly three in the morning, UK time. As it happened, his father was sore and not sleeping well. He was tetchy and wanted an update on Edward's condition. He refused to let his lovely wife give him pain medication or hustle him back to bed without it. George complied as best as he was able. It wasn't like he had a lot of information to report, and he'd already told them about Meg.

Then his littlest brother, Fred, hopped in the mix. It was unclear what he was doing awake at such an hour. Fred had achieved a certain minor celebrity there at home, now that they'd decided to ditch the home tutors and enroll him in the local public school. Though he'd grown up with half of the kids there, he was the only one among them who had spent the last few years living across the pond in America. Somehow, this notoriety had landed Fred a girlfriend named Bianca before he'd even set foot in a single class. Freddy reported that she had splendidly curly black hair, though George had rather large doubts that the teens would be able to get up to much mischief, given their hovering parents. Still, he was Fred's big brother, and as such, he felt obligated to answer the kid's rather urgent (but refreshingly innocent) questions.

By the time he was able to extricate himself from the call, George had a mere five minutes to get himself to Jazz & Java before Poppy locked the doors. It would take at least twenty to work his way through the convoluted streets of Boston, littered as they were with dead-ends and one-ways. Twenty minutes to make it to Poppy. God *damn* it—George was almost certainly going to miss her.

He drove like a bat out of hell anyway, and when he made the last U-turn on Commonwealth Avenue, he was startled to see an inordinate number of people loitering around on the sidewalk. He scanned the crowd but didn't see Poppy. A brown Buick sedan was pulling away from the curb just as he drew level with the café, so he slotted his truck into the spot, killed the engine, and looked around again.

The clusters of students were all laughing and high-spirited. An old van in the spot in front of him had its rear doors spread wide, and three spindly lads in knit rasta caps were loading speakers and amps into the back. Poppy hadn't mentioned there would be live music in the coffee shop tonight, but that certainly seemed to be what had happened. It must have been a madhouse. As he expected, Jazz was closed—all of its interior lights were off and the windows were black.

George got out and locked his doors, glaring at a couple of assholes who were looking a little too covetously at his ride. Judging by the way they moved back, though, his truck would be safe from molestation. George smiled, satisfied that his scary mug had done the trick.

Where *was* Poppy, anyway? She had to still be here somewhere. Based on the look of things, the whole operation had only shut down moments before. People were still dispersing, the band hadn't left…there was no way Poppy would've had enough time to close up shop and then grab a train home. And at this hour, there wasn't a cabbie in sight.

He was wheeling in a circle, searching up and down the street, when he heard it—the unmistakably ugly sound of liquored-up men, bent on destruction. The hairs on the back of his neck rose as he scanned for the source of the jeering. Moving fast along the sidewalk, he finally spotted them across the street. A clutch of idiots, drunk as lords, were advancing with sneering faces on the lone woman standing at the T stop. She was clutching a messenger bag and looking pissed as hell, and George's heart stuttered to a stop when he saw her face. Poppy. *Fuck*. George took off at a dead run, dodging a handful of cars as he raced across the southbound lanes of Comm Ave to get to the T stop in the center, and his woman.

When his feet hit the pavement of the train stop, Poppy's body language was tense and jumpy-looking. George wasn't sure he could predict just *what* she might do. She had been smart enough to back farther away from the knot of men, thereby clearing the high wall that protected the stop from the street, and giving herself an exit if she ended up having to run. George watched as she also eased the strap of her bag crossways across her torso, sliding it behind her so it was out of the way and her hands were free. Her voice, when she spoke, wasn't scared, either—it was furious. A surge of pride filled him. His girl was a tough little cookie.

"What do you dimwits think you're gonna do?" she growled. Her arm flew out toward the sidewalk, gesturing. "You have, like, a hundred witnesses!"

No one appeared to have noticed George's presence yet. One of the morons toward the front of the pack drawled, "There won't be any, once we get on the train."

His Poppy was no fool. She took another healthy step back, and looked ready for flight. Ready for anything, really. They might try to manhandle her onto the next train, but they'd have to catch her first, and Poppy clearly intended to go down swinging. George eased up on her right side, leaving her path of retreat open to the left. After that comment from the loser in front of him, George felt about as big and mean as the Hulk, and just as ready to dismember someone. Poppy might not necessarily need him, but she had him, and he wasn't going to stand by while she fended for herself. She obviously still hadn't realized he was there—Poppy nearly jumped out of her skin when she saw him, poor girl.

"Jesus!" she squeaked. "George! Where'd you come from?"

Without taking his eyes from the group in front of him, he tossed her his keys. "I'm parked right in front of Jazz, and sweetheart, I would love it if you would go lock yourself in my truck right now," he said calmly.

"As if!" she retorted hotly. "I'm not leaving you here alone with these goons!"

The goons in question looked slightly cagier now that George had arrived, but they were still watching the exchange with too much interest.

"Besides, it doesn't matter," Poppy added. "Look."

Sure enough, the headlamps of the oncoming train had appeared up the track, and were steadily trundling closer.

"If you know what's good for you, you'll get on that train without another word," George told the men matter-of-factly. "*Without* her." Had they been sober, they might have heeded his warning a little more closely. Instead, they didn't seem as if they'd given up quite yet. He stepped forward, clenching his fists and putting himself between them and Poppy. They would take her with them over George's dead body. The gesture seemed to be enough to convince the two blokes in the back—they had their fare cards out and ready to swipe before the T had even come to a full stop. And when the train doors slid open with a wheeze, the men herded their friends up the stairs without complaint.

"She's not even worth it, man," the last one muttered as he passed.

George disagreed. When the lights of all three cars had passed and the T was well on its way toward Kenmore Square in a gust of hot, fetid wind, George turned, finally, to gaze at Poppy. She deflated before his eyes, just as if she'd been pricked by a pin.

"You sure have a knack for showing up at just the right time, BL," she said shakily.

"It's a gift," he told her. George glanced down the tracks once more, noticing that the westbound train was heading toward them on the opposite tracks.

"Madam?" he asked, giving her a stiff little bow. "Your chariot awaits." He slung his arm around her narrow shoulders, and turned her toward the street. They trotted across Commonwealth and he led her toward the safety of his pickup truck. George tried very hard not to dwell on what might have happened if he'd been too late, or, God forbid, she'd had another panic attack. For all her bravado, Poppy had been very vulnerable back there. He gritted his teeth. He needed to get her home, damn it, and fast, before he lost his shit altogether. He held the passenger door open.

"Hop in, love. I promise, I'll have you home quicker than you can say knife," he cajoled her. She didn't put up a fight, merely shot him an amused glance before clambering up. He'd purchased the shiny black extended-cab truck the year before. Poppy looked tiny, perched up high in it. It made him grin, the muscles in his neck and shoulders loosening a little at the sight.

He trotted around to his side, slid in, and found Poppy smoothing her palms over the leather seat, looking around in appreciation.

"Sweet ride, dude," she purred.

George felt his chest puff out, like the rooster he apparently was. He loved this blasted truck and was very, very glad she did, too. But there was something else that was more important at the moment.

"Poppy, sweetheart? You all right?"

"I'm fine." Her voice was clipped as she stared out the window. "Just tired, that's all."

"Poppy. Look at me," George commanded. When she did, he asked again, "Are you all right?"

He watched in fascination as her lip quivered just the tiniest bit. But before it could transform into any sign of weakness, she clenched her jaw, stiffened her spine, and said with utter determination, "Yup. Fine and dandy."

Well, if that didn't put the renowned English "stiff upper lip" to shame, George didn't know what did. A smile tugged at his lips. "You're the boss," he told her.

"Then let's roll," she smiled back. And this time, he actually trusted her expression.

"You got it," he murmured, pulling away from the curb.

Poppy directed George across the university's south campus, and on into the Fenway neighborhood. Eventually, they arrived at her building, a massive brick edifice adorned with mossy gray stone around its entryway and upper stories. The building had a lot of character, but it was old, and the courtyard they walked across looked dodgy and neglected in the weak lamp light. Security, to George's mind, seemed nonexistent, and he scowled. How many times had she come home alone at this hour, at risk and undefended?

They traversed the large lobby with its cracked and dirty tile, then ascended what had undoubtedly once been a grand staircase in the back. Poppy's apartment was on the second floor, only a few scuffed wood doors down the hall. George hadn't spent a lot of time envisioning where she lived so much as where she *slept*, but even so he felt a frisson of disappointment. He wasn't exactly sure what he'd been expecting, but it wasn't this. Nothing about it seemed to speak to Poppy's personality.

When they entered the apartment proper, it looked much as the entry led one to anticipate—almost no decoration on the walls and littered with shabby, handed-down furniture. In all likelihood, generations of graduate students had lived and suffered in these spaces, and he had to remind himself that Poppy was, in fact, one of them. George was depressed just trying to imagine her here, day after day—his magnificent, colorful, brave woman, caged here in a virtual gulag. It didn't bear thinking about. His gaze hitched on a framed photo on the wall, of Freud naturally. More nonsensically, that frame was paired with another, this one of Einstein. What on earth could that mean? He refocused on the matter at hand when Poppy flounced onto a frayed sofa with a dispirited groan.

She shrugged, looking around. "It's not pretty, I know. I wasn't able to snag an on-campus place before I moved up here. Subletting a room from Furby was about the only thing I could find on short notice."

"It's charming," George tried weakly. This place would make his brother Edward want to shrivel up and hide in a corner.

"No, it isn't. But it gets the job done, it's close to work and school, and it's not forever."

She looked utterly defeated, the poor lamb. If she'd put in a full day of class and teaching, and had then been on her feet serving a rowdy concert crowd, her feet were likely killing her.

"You stay there," George instructed her. "I'll be right back." He had an idea.

"Not sure I can move anyway," Poppy mumbled, eyeing him curiously.

He slipped into the kitchen he'd noticed, and just as he expected, there was a large plate-drying rack next to the sink. And in the cabinet under it, he found the rectangular plastic basin that often came with them, meant for washing the dishes, he supposed. This one was clean, deep enough for his purposes, and a hideously awful powder blue. He ran the water until it turned hot, set the tub in the sink to fill, and peered around. A row of tiny bottles was lined up along the back of the range and he stepped closer to have a look. Lavender oil, grapefruit oil, peppermint, something purporting to stave off headaches, one whose purpose he could only guess at…and one for relaxation. Perfect. He grabbed the vial, poured a healthy dose into the hot water, then leaned in. Sniffing experimentally at the steam, he realized he'd smelled this scent on her before. Poppy probably went through gallons of the stuff.

While the water ran, he wandered back out to the living room to check on Poppy. She was stretched out on the sofa, her feet propped on the arm and eyes closed. Not wanting to disturb her in case she'd fallen asleep, he drifted over to the stereo setup, looking over the CDs scattered there. George had to smile. This, at least, was all Poppy. There was Elvis of course, in all his Jailhouse Rock glory, lying right on top. But there was also Ella Fitzgerald and Charlie Parker, Billie Holiday…even Edith Piaf. And there was one other name he didn't recognize. When he turned back to her, Poppy was watching him.

"Who's this?" he asked, holding up the case with the modern, distinctive-looking brunette on the cover.

"Madeleine Peyroux. Don't you know her?" Poppy asked.

George shook his head.

"Pop it in, dude. Maybe you'll like it," she smiled, sitting up to remove her shoes and massage her feet.

George cued up the CD and hit play, then stepped back into the kitchen to check on the progress of the water.

"George? What are you doing in there?" she called, amusement rather than suspicion coloring her tone. He grabbed a dishtowel, hoisted the heavy tub out of the sink, and carried it gingerly into the living room, trying not to slosh water everywhere.

Poppy was lying down again. A low, smoky woman's voice was singing smoothly about *dancing her to the end of love*. It was unbelievably erotic. George hesitated, feeling like a caveman for wanting to get Poppy naked, when all she really needed from him was some coddling. Warily, he approached the couch, laying down the towel and setting the basin on top of it.

"Here we are," he told her, avoiding her too-perceptive eyes. "Let's have those feet, sweetheart."

Poppy sat up with a perplexed look, glancing from the water to George and back again.

"Put them in here," he told her, pulling her legs sideways so she would face forward. He reached for the hems of her pants, folding them up as high as he could, then took her ankles in his hands and helped her into the water. George frowned, hoping the water wasn't too hot. It wasn't quite as deep as he wanted, but at least it covered the tops of her small pale feet, and flowed partway up her trim ankles. Her toenails were painted black, but with some kind of sparkly coating, like a night sky full of stars.

"Oh my God," Poppy groaned, slumping back on the couch. "That feels so good. George, you're a *god*."

The singer had shifted into a new song, this one in French. George winced. The combination of the sexy music and Poppy's blissed-out commentary had him hard as a rock. He cleared his throat and stood quickly.

"Be right back," he told her. Maybe not *right* back, but close enough.

Her eyes popped open. "Where are you going now?"

"Thought I'd find you something to eat," he said.

"George, it's okay. I ate at work."

"Tea then?" he asked, a little desperately.

She smiled. "No thanks."

"Something stiffer, then," Mentally he castigated himself for that unfortunate turn of phrase. "Some rum, or, er..."

"George?"

"Hmm?"

"Please sit down."

"Right. Sitting down." He sank down to the floor again, taking each foot in turn out of the water to massage it, moving over her ankles and what he could reach of her calves.

After another couple groans from Poppy that shot straight down his spine, she focused on his face again.

"I thought for a minute you were going to pound those guys, BL," she said cautiously.

A faint smile touched his lips. He probably would have, if he hadn't been so worried for her welfare. George found himself parroting something a client had told him the prior fall, after George had barked at the man's wife a wee bit too brusquely.

"I suppose when one is a hammer, a lot of things tend to look like nails," he retorted.

That hadn't been the first time the sentiment had been applied to George, and likely wouldn't be the last. The only difficulty being that he didn't *feel* like that at all. In his mind, he was more of a gentle giant. And he preferred a bit of softness in return, as when his mum stroked his hair and kissed his cheek when he came for dinner. Or the way his grandmother met the boys with plates of fresh-baked scones whenever they visited her. That was probably his darkest, dirtiest secret, George reflected, the one he would admit to no one—the rough Hughes hound longed for a home and a family of his own. One he could protect and nurture and spoil rotten, and one that would do the same in return for him.

Poppy stared at him, measuring his words and looking unconvinced. But she was clever, his Poppy, and so she deftly changed the subject.

"My faculty advisor is going to deep-six my internship application at the Gardner," she mentioned casually.

"Is that for this summer?"

Poppy nodded, looking away.

"Why?" he asked carefully, trying to keep his tone as neutral as hers. He probably shouldn't offer to beat him up just yet, not after what had happened tonight.

"Mostly because he's a dick," she said forlornly.

"I'm sorry about that." George stroked her ankle bones with his thumbs. His hands were large enough to wrap almost completely around her ankles. "What other programs did you apply for?"

Poppy bit her lip. "Um, that's really the only one. I don't have a prayer of getting into the MFA program. I just…really wanted the one at the Gardner."

George blinked up at her. "You know, for such a practical girl, that was a pretty daft move. You always need a Plan B," he suggested gently.

"I know," she sighed. "I don't know what I was thinking. It was stupid. But…" she closed her eyes and dropped her head back against the couch. "I've been so busy. I can't even think straight anymore. And now it's probably too late to try for anything else. I'm screwed."

George had always refused to believe in giving up before the fight was well and truly over. And in this case, he doubted it was really too late. It was only a matter of working the problem. He wouldn't try to strategize now, though—Poppy seemed too tired for that. But he would definitely add this to the list of things he was intent on fixing.

The water in the basin was cooling, and Poppy's pretty toes were beginning to wrinkle. He lifted her feet out and set them on the towel, then stood to bring the water back into the kitchen.

"George, that was truly amazing," she murmured. It had a note of finality to it, and he expected he was about to be dismissed. It was too soon. Damn it, it was too *soon*.

"My pants got a little damp at the bottom," she added then. "Stay here. I'm going to go change, and I'll be right back."

"Sure," he told her, spirits lifting with his reprieve. "Are you sure you don't want any tea?"

"Yup, just hang tight." And then she was up and moving down the hall. He waited only long enough to note which door led to her bedroom, and then he went to dump the tub out and set it to dry.

When Poppy returned, George had to smile at her outfit. If this was her version of *slipping into something a little more comfortable*...he could totally get with the program. Poppy had left her blouse as it was, but had donned a loose pair of cut-off sweatpants on the bottom. She was too cute for words. And her suddenly exposed legs were like something out of an old pinup magazine. He wavered, wondering if he was really going to be able to keep his paws to himself.

She didn't make it easy on him, naturally. George had parked it on one end of her ghastly couch to wait for her. When Poppy slouched onto the other end, then pulled up one leg so she could turn to face him...he had a rather exceptional view of her inner thighs. And her apparent ignorance of his discomfiture only made him more deranged. He *wanted* her to know what he was going through. He wanted her to have the same damn problem.

George leaned forward and eased his hands up her legs to her parted thighs. She was even softer than she looked, and she didn't flinch or pull away. But she'd also had a long day, so George tore his eyes from her legs to check her expression. One look at the smoky desire hazing her eyes though, and he knew he could have her, right here, right now. But rather immediately, it felt like it was moving too fast, and George had the sudden urge to slow things down. Leaning back, he pulled her legs straight over his lap and began massaging them again, from her arches and toes, to her lovely curved calves, to her delectable thighs. He allowed himself to linger, to notice the feel of her skin, and the shape of her muscles, and the ink scattered around.

George had never been much for tattoos, himself—that had always been Edward's thing—but it was hard to resist the lure of a roadmap into Poppy's psyche. He was terribly taken with the designs she'd chosen, and where she'd chosen to place them. Tracing an unsteady fingertip over her ankle, encircled by the image of a dainty chain and a tiny heart pendant inscribed with a "W", he decided to ask.

"Are they all just to be pretty? Or do they mean something special to you?"

She smiled. "They mean things."

"Such as?" he pressed on the little heart, looking up at her.

She looked down at the anklet tattoo. "At the time, I felt chained by the weight of the expectations and love of my family." *Ah.* Poppy's last name was Whitlock—"W" for Whitlock.

"And this?" There was a sun design directly above the chain. He rubbed one rough fingertip over it.

"Suns can represent the light of knowledge and insight. Once I got to college, I realized that I had more choices that I thought. I could...determine my destiny, you know what I mean?"

"Mm-hmm," he agreed. George had a little experience with just that sort of thing, himself.

His eyes had gone roving, though, and snagged on another bit of ink just peeking out from under the hem of her shorts, high up on her other leg. He flicked his glance up to hers in inquiry. Poppy hiked her shorts up a couple inches higher, and looked a little sly. When he looked back down, George was confronted with the sight of a very realistic, lacy band of a garter. Around her upper thigh. Dear God. His throat went dry. Leaning forward, he smoothed his palm over the hot, silken skin there, fascinated, wanting to kiss it.

Poppy's hands sunk into his hair, she made what was probably the most erotic sound on earth, and he was a goner. George grabbed her hips, yanked her flat under him, and covered her with his body. When he sank his head down to have a taste of her lips, she was already there, clicking their teeth together, and tangling her tongue with his. It wasn't elegant, but it didn't seem to matter. They were inhaling each other with desperate hunger, peppering mouths and faces and necks with greedy, open-mouthed kisses. George searched out the shape of her hip with his hand, the weight of her breasts, the flat plane of her stomach. Poppy had worked her hands up under his t-shirt, and was pressing her cool palms all over his back and ribcage. The feel of her was driving him insane. He switched hands, holding the weight of himself off of her with his other arm, so he could grip her leg, right over the garter tattoo. His red-blooded male brain was flooded with images of what exactly that was going to look like, once he'd divested her of her clothes. He pushed higher, fingertips touching the edge of her panties, then sliding beneath.

George heard two things in quick succession. It was a wonder, really, that he could hear anything at all over the roaring in his ears, and the pounding of his heart. But clear as the sound of a drill in an empty house, he heard Poppy gasp when he stroked the place where her leg met her body. He wanted to hear *that* sound again. Unfortunately, he also heard another sound, and that was a key in the lock of the front door. *Fuck.*

He wrenched his hand from her shorts and yanked them both upright, just as Poppy's flatmate breezed into the apartment. A quick glance confirmed that they both looked disheveled as hell, but since Philby was worse, George presumed he wouldn't notice.

"What's up," the man said, spotting them. He strode over, and every cell in George's body screamed in frustration and denial.

"You guys get wasted?" Nathan inquired, looking them over. "You look like shit."

"Naw, I think that was you," Poppy retorted bitterly.

Any sign of the erection George had been sporting was long gone, so he he fell back on generations of good breeding and stood up to shake the other man's hand. Philby didn't seem to notice.

"So, Pop-Tart, I heard you guys had *Sweet Jamaica* at Jazz tonight," he said.

"We did," Poppy agreed, shooting George a glance. It might've meant *sit down*, or it might have meant *beat him to a pulp*. It was hard to tell. He stayed standing.

"That's cool," Nathan commented. When he looked as if he might plop down into one of the armchairs, Poppy snarled in outrage.

"Furby!" she barked.

"What?"

"Get lost!" Poppy yelled.

"A'right," the other man slurred. "I see how it is." He turned on his heel with a dramatic roll of his bloodshot eyes, and moved unsteadily away.

George stood in the center of the living room scowling at Philby's back, fists clenched as the other man shambled down the short hall to his bedroom. As if he didn't have a care in the world.

"BL?" Poppy had waited a moment before asking, helpfully giving him a minute to try to regulate his blood pressure.

He turned back to her. "That's twice that fucker has interrupted us like that. It's not cricket!" George complained. "I'm beginning to think that he's doing it on purpose."

"He's not, I swear," Poppy reassured him. "He really *is* that oblivious."

"Yeah, well, next time he does it, I'm going to have to rearrange his face," George muttered, pissy as a fourteen-year-old girl.

Poppy let out an amused little snort that, when he glared at her, turned into a full-blown spate of breathless giggles. George had to smile—the sound was too infectious not to. He also had to acknowledge that he was maybe being just a touch unreasonable. Philby was a queer fish, all right, but he seemed harmless enough, and not in the least bit interested in Poppy. But honestly, how much sexual frustration was one bloke expected to endure? Much more of this and he was likely to boil over like a bloody volcano.

Poppy patted the couch cushion next to her, and George grudgingly settled in. After a few moments, she lay sideways, her head on the armrest and her legs draped across his lap.

She murmured drowsily, "I bet this didn't go the way you expected."

"I had no expectations, love," He rested his hand across her pale, delicate little foot, and within moments, she was out cold.

George didn't know what it was about this woman, but there was just something *more* about Poppy. He'd always fancied brunettes, but with Poppy, you never knew which rich color of hair she was going to show up with next—you just knew no one else in the room would have it. The fact that she routinely wore it twisted up at the back of her head merely drove him crazier. He was forever fantasizing about releasing it and watching it tumble down over a variety of body parts, both his and hers. Her nails weren't just painted some soft barely-there pink, they were metallic navy blue. Or black with that glitter coating that made them look like little ovals of galaxies on her fingertips. Her skin wasn't only a spectacular, smooth cream that George could kiss for hours, it was littered with glorious, mysterious little symbols—each small tattoo a key to a secret about Poppy that he very much wanted to unravel. And her clothes...definitely *more*. A style from some other era, like an extra-foxy Rosie the Riveter, destined to be painted on the side of a bomber plane. George never would have guessed it of himself, but he adored the fact that she didn't look like everyone else, and he wanted to unwrap her like a birthday present every time he saw her. Poppy was a bit of a perfectionist with her appearance, come to think of it—her hair and nails and makeup perfect, her clothes impeccably pressed and arranged, and her tidiness made him a bit mad with longing. He'd never wanted to mess up another human being more in his life, and he'd prefer to do it in a bed. For a few long weekends, give or take. Lately, the women he'd run across had seemed as dull as ditchwater. Not Poppy. This one was living in technicolor, and George had no idea how he'd ever found anything else attractive.

Reluctantly, he extricated himself from under her legs and pulled the ratty blanket off the back of a chair to cover her. George left her on the nod, curled on the sofa like some dazzling fairy princess trapped in the mundane world. With one last glance, he let himself out of her flat, locking the door behind him. He had time, he told himself. Now that he'd found her, he had time.

Chapter Five

AFTER GEORGE'S HEROICS two weeks before, Poppy felt like she owed him one. She'd managed to meet up with him again a handful of times, for quick lunches and coffees in between all her other commitments. They met for a drink after work, and took a stroll through the Athenaeum. But, while the dates scratched the itch a little bit, they mostly left her feeling unsatisfied, wanting more. So when George told Poppy he had arranged to take her to one of his favorite places today, a tiny contemporary art institute in Kenmore Square that Poppy had never even heard of, she jumped at the chance. They could spend the morning there, since she had no classes on Saturdays and hadn't scheduled any teaching sessions. She was working the lunch shift at Jazz today instead of breakfast. After that, she would have just enough time to get home and get ready for tonight's gala. The Gardner's annual charity auction was being held in the courtyard of the museum, and all the internship applicants knew it was imperative they attend this event. Not only would they get some critical face-time with the people making decisions about the summer interns and their research projects, but Sarge would be there, too, in all her snooty, judgmental glory. No

applicant wanted to be noted as absent, and every one of them
desperately wanted the chance to shine.

In a moment of weakness on the way to the institute, Poppy had
begged George to go with her. The thought of the auction terrified
her, knowing that Mini was intent on stonewalling her internship
application. And, for some reason, BL just made her feel steady.
Sane. She'd known the man two damn weeks, and already Poppy
needed him. It was bizarre. But she didn't have much time to wallow
in her relief when George agreed, because with his usual efficiency,
he had found a spot to park his truck only a block from the institute.
They entered through an unassuming, painted red door sporting a
small engraved brass plaque, then scanned the pamphlets piled on a
table in the foyer. The institute was showing a large photographic
exhibit this month, a series of black and white pictures profiling
restorations of historic buildings. It spanned the years after the first
world war up to the present day ravages terrorism had wrought on
architectural treasures. Right up George's alley—and, Poppy found,
amazing to her also. George made a fascinating companion. With
his construction background, he was able to lend incredible insight
into what was happening in each series. They wandered through the
exhibit, engaged with what they were seeing in a way that felt new
and refreshing to Poppy. She didn't have to interpret anything
through the lens of her studies—she only had to enjoy it. And that
was a rare gift she doubted BL understood he was giving her.

When an eager docent spotted them, he moved quickly to strike up
a conversation. His name was Brendan, and he didn't seem the least
bit affronted by George's Bruins hat, or Poppy's red Doc Martens.
"I'd ask you guys if you were enjoying yourselves, but you so
obviously are, it seems a little silly to point it out," Brendan smiled.
"Have you visited us before?"

"I haven't," Poppy told him. "I can't believe I didn't know you were
here."

"Yeah—I keep telling Kathleen we need to do something about that front door," he laughed. "It's a little forbidding if you don't know what's inside."

George pulled himself away from the placard he'd been reading. "I wasn't sure you would be able to match the level of that show you had last fall," he commented. "The one with the paintings by the Holocaust survivors?"

Brendan nodded earnestly. "Oh, yes, that one was one of our favorites."

"I can see why," George agreed. "But this exhibit is terrific, too. You totally outdid yourselves."

Brendan beamed. "Thanks, man. I'll tell Kathleen you said that. She's the director," he added in explanation.

"Well, I think you certainly made one new convert today," George said, elbowing Poppy with a wink.

"What do you have coming up this summer?" she inquired. The docent was so friendly, and clearly loved his job. She wanted to throw him a bone.

"Oh, it's going to be great. We scored this modern watercolorist. He's excellent. Does these large white fields of parchment, with just a little vivid slice of a person or scene somewhere in the space. They really make you want to know the rest of the story," Brendan enthused. "The best way I can describe him is that he's sort of a cross between a graffiti artist and a cave painter," he laughed. "And then city sanitation came and covered three-quarters of the design with white paint. So the next person who finds it is dying to know what happened, what the full picture looked like." He lit up talking about it, and his delight was infectious. Poppy knew she'd be back to see the exhibit the minute it opened.

"Well, well," George commented, staring pointedly at her. "That sounds remarkably like *someone's* graduate thesis."

Poppy flushed, and Brendan's eyes darted back and forth between them, suddenly intent.

"I wonder if they have summer internships here?" BL continued, his expression turning sly.

"We do! We just started them last year," Brendan interjected, picking up on George's direction. "Do you know someone who might be interested?" His question was unnecessary, because he was already staring at Poppy.

"It's possible that this woman is in the market," George agreed, smirking. "That is, if it isn't too late."

"It's totally not too late," Brendan assured them. All business now, he turned to her. "Where are you in school?" he asked.

"I'm in the History of Art and Architecture program at BU, but I'll get a museum studies certificate when I graduate next year, too."

"And your undergrad?"

"I have a B.F.A. in museum studies from the University of Florida," she told him.

"Who's your advisor this year?" Brendan pressed, like a dog with a bone now.

"Stephen Cooper," Poppy offered. He might not be helpful in many other ways, but Mini was still good for the occasional name drop.

Brendan grimaced, clearly familiar with the professor's reputation. However, it didn't seem to blunt his enthusiasm—he was fairly quivering with it.

"I have to tell you, we're small and our program is pretty new. We don't get too many applicants of your caliber." He snorted, "Or any, really. Kathleen is going to freaking lose it." Then, in a conspiratorial whisper, he confided, "You didn't hear this from me, but I bet if you asked, she'd probably even pay you."

George raised an amused eyebrow at Poppy. "Oh my," he said. "That does sound good."

Poppy's heart was pounding, but she tried to hold it together. "Your deadline has to be soon, though, right?"

"You have till the end of the month," Brendan explained. "But that's no big deal. How soon do you think you could get your transcripts sent over? I mean, if you're interested." He was trying to keep his cool, too, but the man's excitement was palpable.

Shooting an arch look at George, Poppy promised she would call the transcript office first thing in the morning. Brendan whipped out his cell phone to take down her contact information, then hurried away to scan the application and email it to her.

"I have to go tell Kathleen," Brendan said, by way of farewell. "She'll call you as soon as we get your application and your transcripts," he cried over his shoulder, disappearing across the gallery at a fast clip.

George stood there, chest puffed out and hands in his pockets, looking smug.

"You dirty rat," Poppy said, smacking him in the chest. "You planned this, didn't you?"

"Not all of it," he admitted, laughing. "Mostly it was luck. But I had a feeling." He hooked a heavy, muscled arm around her and pulled her closer.

Poppy had to admit, an exhibit that was a cross between cave painting and graffiti sounded just about *perfect* for her thesis. It seemed too good to be true, and there was only one little hang up.

"I hope they don't require a faculty recommendation," she worried, looking up at him.

"He didn't mention one. But listen, do you even like it here? Does it seem like a good fit?" he asked, knocking the brim of his hat gently on the crown of her head to get her attention.

"I love it here," Poppy admitted. "Like—*really* love it here."

"Then the rest will come," George intoned, wrapping his arms tighter around her. Poppy let him hold her, there in the center of the exhibit gallery. Let his warmth and confidence seep into her soul. Brendan *had* seemed to like her, a lot. She let herself, just a teensy bit, begin to hope.

WHEN GEORGE PICKED her up for the auction later that evening, Poppy opened her door to the mind-boggling sight of him in a tuxedo. She'd expected some sort of ill-fitting suit, not the exquisite, bespoke set of black tie evening wear confronting her, or the hunk of virile manhood wearing it.

"Hooooo-lee shit, 007, look at you!" Poppy breathed, agape.

George smiled serenely. "I could say the same about you, sweetheart. You look smashing."

Poppy smoothed her hands down the front of her vintage burgundy velvet gown, suddenly nervous. The dress crisscrossed on her torso in gathered folds, with narrow shoulders tied in little satin bows. The back draped low, and the hem hit high on her ankles at the front, with a slight train in back. She'd picked it up at a consignment store, and wondered if that was obvious.

"Really? Thanks," she replied uncertainly.

She studied him. His self-possession, and the way the penguin suit tracked his muscular frame—that was no ordinary rent-a-tux, not by a long shot. BL clearly owned the hell out of those threads. He looked...*comfortable* in them.

"Shall we?" he asked, holding out his hand to her.

Poppy slipped her palm into his, and George walked her out to a gleaming black BMW parked on the street in front of her building.

"Um, seriously?" she squawked, incredulous as George hit a button to unlock the car with a chirp, then held the passenger door wide for her. He stood patiently by while she slid gingerly into the deep bucket seat. His eyes took in every detail of her outfit, from the rhinestone clip in her hair to the calf-hair heels on her feet.

"You like the car?" he asked absently, then leaned in to detangle her when Poppy's black shawl got mixed up with the seat belt. He didn't wait for an answer, though, only shut her in and walked around the front of the car to the driver's side. Poppy glanced quickly around at the shiny burled-wood trim of the console and doors, then ran her hand across the soft tan leather of the seat.

"These your wheels?" she asked dubiously, once George had tucked himself into the seat beside her.

He chuckled. "No," he said, as if he didn't look like a perfect men's cologne ad right now. As if the very idea of him owning this car was preposterous. "This is Ed's car. He let me borrow it tonight. I thought it might be easier for you to get in and out of than my truck," he explained. "Since you're all dressed up."

Well. That was considerate. "I see," Poppy answered, staring at the sophisticated man beside her. "Not too shabby."

His gaze raked over her again, leaving a burning trail of lava in its wake. "Do my eyes deceive me, or are you wearing leopard print heels, baby doll?" George inquired.

"Oh. Yeah," Poppy said, lifting her hem a little and turning her foot so he could see the shoe better. "Do you think they're too much?" She'd been uncharacteristically worried about that. But she wanted the Gardner internship so much, and Sarge didn't seem the type to appreciate leopard-print *anything*.

He shook his head, gripping the wheel and staring down at them. He didn't seem quite able to look away, as a matter of fact. Poppy laughed nervously.

"BL?" Poppy asked. "Do you...*like* them?"

In answer, a low purring growl rolled from George's throat. She wouldn't have thought a human could make such a sexy sound if she hadn't just heard it with her own ears. George looked like he'd like to pounce on her, and Poppy clutched the small satin evening bag in her lap a little tighter. George raised his eyes and stared at her, then slowly leaned in to press his lips to hers.

Next thing she knew, though, he was checking his mirrors and pulling on to the street, steering the gorgeous heap of fine German engineering like he'd been born to do it.

"We should get going," he murmured, the corners of his mouth ticking up in a devilish slant. So he'd noticed how flustered she was. Terrific.

Poppy blinked at him, trying to process this new, debonair side of George. Finally, unable to believe what she was witnessing, she blurted out, "Who *are* you, and what have you done with George?"

He chuckled, another sexy sound she'd like to file away for posterity, but he didn't take his eyes off the road. "Is it so hard to believe, then?" he asked her. "Me in a tux?"

"It's not just you in a tux," Poppy tried to explain. "It's you looking—and acting—like you were born in a tux. What gives?"

"What do you mean?" he inquired, but it was obvious he was stalling. The man had gone from charming to uncomfortable in seconds, and that was very interesting indeed.

Poppy studied him. "You're not just a contractor, are you?" she asked softly.

He was silent for long moments. "No," he finally admitted.

Poppy waited for the rest, but nothing else seemed forthcoming. "And?" she demanded. "Who are you *really*?"

George seemed to sag a little in his seat, as if resigned to having to tell her. "And...I'm also the second son of the Earl of Westbroke," he muttered.

Poppy gaped at him, too stunned to even laugh. You couldn't make this shit up.

"BL, do you mean to tell me –" she began, stunned.

"That I'm the spare heir?" he inquired, cutting her off. "Yes," he said. "Of course, there are two others, should something untoward befall me." At that, George seemed to regain his composure, because he shot one fast look at her, eyebrows raised. Poppy had the sensation that she'd inadvertently stepped into someone else's murder-mystery game. Thankfully, his expression let her know he found this as amusing as she was starting to. "I'm the grandson of a baron on my mum's side, too, but Edward has the courtesy title. He's a viscount. I'm just *The Honourable George Hughes.*"

Poppy's wits were beginning to return to her. "So what you're saying is, you're essentially Harry," she confirmed, smiling at his profile.

He smirked. "Essentially. Without being a bloody prince." He kept driving.

Poppy paused. "Does anyone ever call you *Number Two?*" she blurted.

George snorted. "I'm sorry, you cheeky little chit, was that an Austin Powers impression you just did?"

"It's Doctor Evil, doofus," she corrected him. "So? Do they?"

"Literally not a one, dollface. And don't you start, either," he demanded, shooting her a look he probably meant to be threatening.

Poppy leaned back, smiling coyly through the windshield. "Don't worry," she assured George. "You'll always be BL to me." It hadn't taken George long to demand to know what his nickname stood for. And once she'd convinced him she wasn't comparing him to fat Elvis, he seemed okay with it. That was a good thing, too, because the moniker was so fixed in Poppy's brain at this point, he wasn't likely to ever dislodge it.

"Got that right," he growled.

THEY VALET PARKED his brother's car and slowly made their way through the glittering clusters of guests to the famous courtyard of the museum. George stopped at the bar to grab them two flutes of champagne, leisurely led Poppy on a circuit of the space, then leaned against one of the stone arches to the side, surveying the attendees. The other internship candidates were easy enough to spot. Twenty-somethings in borrowed or handed-down formalwear, all bearing identical expressions of anxiety. All valiantly trying to plaster pleasant, capable-looking smiles over their terror. It took a certain amount of bravery, wading into these types of events despite their nerves, especially when the individuals here could make or break their fragile, fledgling careers. It was a good thing there was a cash bar. Many of them would want to knock back some liquid courage, but their empty student pockets would probably prevent them from over-imbibing and embarrassing themselves. Poppy sipped carefully at her own glass, trying to look like she did this sort of thing all the time. George clearly did.

"Oh, God, it's Sarge," Poppy muttered under her breath, noticing the society maven heading their way after only an hour of mingling. Of course George heard her.

"Who?" he asked, too loud and looking around. When he didn't immediately spot a paunchy older man in a uniform, he looked back down at Poppy, baffled.

But Sarge was upon them then, and there was no time to explain. She sailed to a stop and levelled at them the coldest smile Poppy had ever seen.

"Ms. Whitlock, yes?"

"Yes," Poppy agreed, shaking Sarge's limp, manicured hand.

Before Poppy could introduce her date, the woman turned to George, taking him in with a glance. Her gaze sharpened, seeing more than Poppy would've liked. She extended her hand and proclaimed, "Claire Sargent-Chaffee. I'm the internship director here at the Gardner."

Poppy cleared her throat as George took the woman's hand. "This is my friend George Hughes." BL raised an eyebrow at her, no doubt questioning her use of the term "friend." But Sarge pulled his attention back to herself.

"And are you fond of our little collection, Mr. Hughes?" She was resplendent in her long black sequined gown, her strawberry blonde hair pulled into a perfect chignon at the back of her head. She looked like a mannequin.

"You seem to have several very nice pieces," he replied neutrally. Oh, he was smooth. Poppy doubted he'd seen a single thing hanging in this place, given that he'd spent the evening so far alternately trying to urge her into dark corners, and shooting hungry looks down her décolletage.

"Will you two be bidding in the auction later?" Sarge inquired, looking between them with a condescending smirk. Turning to George, she added, "I'm sure Ms. Whitlock has told you of our efforts to bring *Assumption, bleu et vert* here for the fall season. That is, after all, what brings us all here this evening."

No, Ms. Whitlock had certainly *not* told him that, since she had no idea that's what the Gardner was trying to do. What was more, Poppy had never even heard of *Assumption, bleu et vert*. Was it a painting? A sculpture? For all she knew, it could be a twenty-inch-long necklace. She tried to school her expression, which she assumed was currently bordering on panic. This was something she should know. Admitting she didn't could lose her any last chance she had at the internship. Poppy couldn't shake the sense that she'd been purposely excluded from some important loop.

"Naturally," George replied, unimpressed and almost indifferent. "But I'm afraid we'll have to wait until next time to bid. We both have very early mornings tomorrow, and can't stay quite that long, even for such a worthy cause." He made them both sound terribly important. Poppy had been intending to stay until the bitter end, but she had to admit his way sounded much better. No matter how she tried, Ms. Sargent-Chaffee seemed to despise her, and right now she couldn't wait to leave. She was mortally embarrassed that this evil woman was making her look like an idiot in front of George. George, who had turned out to be an aristocrat, likely rich and certainly cultured, and belonged here more than Poppy ever would. Poppy, of the auto parts Whitlocks—it didn't have much of a ring to it.

"What a shame," Sarge murmured, but her attention had already wandered. With a little wave, she acknowledged an older couple making a beeline for her across the party. "If you'll excuse me," she said offhandedly, already gliding away in search of deeper pockets.

"What a ghastly woman," George muttered after she departed. He wiped his hand roughly down his thigh, as if to erase any vestige of her touch. Poppy adored him so much in that moment, she actually thought she *might* let him herd her into a secluded corner. God knew she wanted to kiss the daylights out of him. In his tuxedo, his bulk and clean-cut good looks made him seem like some kind of aristocratic spy.

"What do you say we blow this taco stand?" she asked him, suddenly eager to get him alone.

"No thanks," he replied casually. "I'm not ready to give you up quite yet." He took a measured sip of his champagne.

"We could go to my place instead," she offered, hoping she wasn't *too* transparent.

"Now that," he agreed, "Is a plan I can get behind. Let's roll."

GEORGE WAS NO slouch. Whatever he slipped the valet got them Edward's car back in a hurry, and he navigated the streets back to Poppy's apartment with alacrity. With his usual ease, he found an unmetered spot to park Edward's car, then ushered her through the lobby and up the stairs like he was shepherding her through an elegant cocktail party. However, since they'd already *done* that part of the evening, Poppy was getting impatient to reach the *next* part.

It wasn't until her apartment door swung shut behind them that Poppy got a good look at BL's face. Well, hot damn. *Someone* was in an even bigger hurry than she was. His expression looked like a match had dropped into a vat of turpentine. It was incendiary. He followed her to the living room, coming up warm and solid behind her. Poppy paused in the middle of the floor, and George leaned his head down to drop a soft kiss on the back of her neck. With feather-light fingertips, he moved one dress strap aside, planted more kisses along the top of her shoulder, then trailed a line of fire down her spine as his fingers traced the deep U at the back of her dress. Poppy wanted to think it was because she was a tiny bit tipsy and not because she was a helpless, emotional head case, but she had no defense against gentleness from a man like George. A desperate sound she would rather not examine emerged from her throat, and behind her, George grunted in acknowledgement of it.

His lips brushed the shell of her ear. "Ask me to stay, Poppy," he murmured. His hand cupped her shoulder, impossibly warm against the bare skin there. "Don't make me leave."

Her mind spun. She shouldn't be doing this. She had no time for a relationship, and he deserved better than having to talk her off the ledge every time she lost her shit. But God, BL was very hard to say no to. She couldn't remember the last guy she'd dated, and she'd certainly never been with a man who could kiss like he did.

"Please stay, Mr. Hughes," she breathed. And then, horrifyingly, she began to tear up. She turned and gave him a shaky smile.

"You okay?" he asked, noticing her face immediately. He frowned, and started to back away.

"BL," she said, tentatively. "After the week I've had, and that damn charity party…and *Ms. Sargent-Chaffee*…" Poppy trailed off, resting her hands on his burly chest and trying to gather her thoughts.

He stayed quiet, waiting for her to finish. Prepared, it seemed, for whatever she might say. He covered her hands with his own large ones, holding them in place against his steadily beating heart.

The weight of other people's expectations had always been the hardest burden for her. Trying to be *her*, under the mantle of all that, could be so difficult sometimes. Poppy pushed the rest out in a rush. "I don't know if I can be what you're expecting right now," she confessed. George would expect someone wild. Sexy and confident. Worthy of her leopard-print shoes.

"Do you want this?" he inquired, cutting to the heart of things as usual.

"Yeah. I do," she admitted. "I'm just…" She shook her head. *I'm just lame*, she wanted to say.

George's face was intense as he gazed down at her. "Poppy, you don't need to trot out some dog and pony show just for my benefit. All I want is *you*, however you want to be."

Relief swamped her. Of course he would say that. George was apparently the perfect man, who always had the perfect thing to say.

"Okay," she whispered, swaying toward him again. His arms wrapped around her instantly, feeling warm and safe, solid and steadfast. Poppy knew she was falling fast and hard, and that she was a fool for doing it. She had no illusions that a guy like George was in the market for something long-term, and she certainly didn't have much to offer at this point in her life, either. Still, it felt nice to pretend.

Poppy melted into him, arms slipping around his waist as she went up on her toes to press kisses along his jaw and neck. George closed his eyes and ran his palms up and down her back, worshiping the curve of her spine, and all the exposed skin back there. When he felt the wet warmth of her tongue licking up his neck, his eyes flew open again. Poppy smiled.

George's head swiveled to take in their surroundings. She watched his eyes sweep the room, registering Furby's large, tattered gray sweatshirt discarded on the arm of the couch and the dog-eared pages of a music score spread across the coffee table. Poppy had a roommate—a large, indolent male cohabiter who might stagger in with other drunk and shiftless men at any moment. They seemed to realize that fact at the same moment.

"Not here," he growled. He leaned down to grab the shoes she'd slipped off, then wrapped his other arm around her waist, lifted her against his shoulder, and hauled her down the short hall toward her bedroom. Dutifully, she pointed out the correct door, praying Furby was anywhere but in the next room. Poppy had a feeling George wasn't going to accept a meek and silent performance from her tonight, no matter what he claimed.

Once he closed and locked her bedroom door, George slid off her glasses and set them aside on her night table. She switched on her small bedside lamp, and his hands returned to her face, palms warm as he cupped her cheeks and met her eyes. Then his fingers were rooting around in the hair piled at the back of her head, searching for the clip that held it all together. When he found it, it took only seconds before his nimble fingertips figured out how to release it, and then Poppy's hair was falling, settling around her shoulders in a silky wave. She was glad, in that moment, that she hated hairspray and never used it if she could help it, because George's hands were smoothing her hair down, and his face looked captivated. Holding her head gently, he leaned in to kiss her, then pulled back, still staring at her mouth.

"What color is your hair? I mean, if you didn't do anything to it?" he asked her.

Poppy's instinct was to tense up at the inquiry. But there was no subtext in his tone, no hint of condemnation or disapproval. So instead of deflecting like she normally would with a comment like "Wouldn't you like to know?", she just...answered him.

"Dark brown," she replied.

"Like your eyes," George mused.

Poppy made a small sound of agreement in her throat. She wished he would stop looking at her lips, stop talking only inches from her lips, and instead start kissing her again.

"Like chocolate," he continued huskily.

Oh. Well. That was...George leaned down and starting kissing her neck, his tongue doing wicked things in the neighborhood of her ear. So, she murmured her agreement.

He pulled back slightly to assess her, and every inch of her skin screamed in protest. But then a corner of his mouth tipped up in what had to be the sexiest half-smile she'd ever seen.

"With a delicious candy coating," he added, looking proud of himself.

Poppy was startled as his words filtered into the haze of her brain. She certainly had never heard it put quite that way before, and she tried to think of some suitable comment that was more inventive than a fervent *thank you*. But George was already moving on, slipping the straps of her velvet gown off her shoulders, then reaching around to unzip the small zipper at her back so he could rid her of the dress altogether. With a heavy swoosh, it slithered over her hips and fell down around her ankles in a shimmering dark red puddle. George's large, broad hands gripped her hips, and finally, *finally*, he was kissing her hungrily, his expert tongue searching out hers to tangle with. He wrenched away too quickly and dove for her neck, breathing in her skin with an enormous lung-filling inhale.

"George, that's kind of weird," she giggled.

He pulled back to stare at her, affronted. "Are you fucking kidding me? You smell bloody awesome all the time, love, and I've been on my best behavior for weeks!"

Poppy laughed out loud, unable to resist. "*That* was your best behavior?"

He growled, giving her a frank, top-to-bottom perusal. "Yes. But I find I am inclined to outdo myself." He bent again to suck and bite his way down her neck to her shoulder.

Too late, Poppy remembered what kind of gear she'd had to wear under the backless dress tonight. Lascivious, it was not. Luckily, George appeared amused to find that she was wearing an ugly, utilitarian *thing* on top, an odd rig of a brassiere with zero aesthetic appeal. He was clearly perplexed by its construction, though, and had no flipping clue how to divest her of it. Skin-colored and smooth like a corset in the front, it had a web of satiny ribbons crisscrossing low on her spine behind, and held her breasts in place without being seen above the plunging back of a dress. It even had little snaps to keep it from slipping free from the shoulders of a gown (not that she ever remembered to use them)—it was a wonder of design, when you thought about it.

George couldn't have cared less. He tucked his fingers under two of the ribbons, ran them around her ribcage to her abdomen, and discovered the small clip holding them together right at her navel. He slipped that free, but wasn't any closer to getting it off of her. Poppy watched his baffled frown and decided to have mercy. With a little understanding smile, she relented. Reaching between her breasts, she undid a tiny line of hooks that he obviously hadn't noticed, then peeled the contraption off her body and dropped it to the side. Free of the constraint, Poppy had never felt more feminine in her life—all soft skin and gentle curves, designed to drive a man wild. It certainly seemed to be working on *this* man. He stepped closer and was on her in the space of a heartbeat, his palms cupping her breasts and thumbs toying with her nipples. Hot hands. Rough fingers. Chilly room. Poppy shivered, and arched into his touch with a sigh.

"I'm keen as mustard for you, you know that, right?" George whispered.

"If that means you like me, then I like you too, BL," she answered with a smile. "But I'd like you even better if you had no clothes on."

With a groan and one last hungry sweep of his tongue through her mouth, George wrenched back from her. Moving efficiently, he stripped off his jacket and waistcoat, then bent to shuck his shoes and socks and kick them away. He went to work unknotting his bowtie, while Poppy attacked his shirt buttons and waist band. They had him bare as the day he was born in two minutes flat.

"Poppy, love, I can't wait," he gasped out, slotting words between kisses, between burning licks at her neck and breasts. "I've been dreaming of this for weeks."

"BL," Poppy interjected. "Shut your pie hole."

He pulled back and blinked at her in stunned disbelief. Poppy softened her tone.

"*I mean*, you don't have to explain. I get it," she explained. But lest he lose sight of the endgame, she reached forward to cup his erection, then gave it a gentle squeeze.

George definitely picked up on her urgency, because he didn't bother with finesse, just yanked down her panties, gathered her tight against him, and backed to the edge of the mattress. Once his legs hit the side, he dropped back across her bed, pulling her down with him. He probably meant to break her fall with his body, but given how hard the muscles in his chest and thighs were, it wasn't the softest of landings. Poppy's head whirled at how fast she'd ended up straddling BL, but she supposed now was as good a time as any for him to earn his nickname.

"Wait," he said, shifting his large frame higher up the bed, and carrying her with him.

"No," Poppy told him, though she tried to be nice. To emphasize her point, she gave him a nice slow slide of her body against his groin, just to prove how ready for him she was. There was no doubt at all he was ready for her—she didn't think she'd ever felt a man as hard as he was. They could mess with foreplay later, but right now, they had pretty earnest business to attend to.

Poor George. Maybe that hadn't been a nice move, after all. He squeezed his eyes shut, and clenched his jaw. His hands dug into her hips, where he gripped her a bit too tightly. Without her glasses, it was hard to be sure at this distance, but she thought she saw his Adam's apple bob up and down as George swallowed. It gave her a charge, having this much of an effect on a dude as strong and unemotional as George. But what was it they said? *Still waters run deep.*

"No, really, hang on a minute, love," he said again. Poppy leaned down over him, brushing her breasts against his chest and kissing him deeply. Her heart was pounding and her breath was already coming hard. She didn't have time to dillydally. She felt George fall into the moment, but all too soon his muscles were tensing up again. "Poppy," he gasped insistently. "Seriously, wait."

"What's wrong, BL?" she asked, bracing herself against his chest and peering down at him. It was one thing to play the seductress, but it wasn't much fun with an unwilling mark. Just so he didn't get the idea of giving her the long version, though, she wriggled languorously against him.

He shook his head, clearly trying to stay focused. "We need protection," he breathed, taking her ass in his big hands and pressing her against his lap, right where it counted. "Right this bloody second."

Of course. What was she thinking? That had been indescribably dumb of her.

"Where is it?" she asked. If George didn't have anything with him, Poppy might, but she couldn't say for certain how old the condoms might be. She'd rather rely on him being stocked and up-to-date.

"Inside jacket pocket," he directed breathlessly. He let out a choked sound when she lifted herself off of him to crawl to the end of the bed. When Poppy turned back, victorious at discovering not one, but three condoms in the magic pocket, George was propped up on his arms, drinking in every move she made. He was a specimen, all right, with his bulging biceps and broad, hard chest. The pose might have been amusing on any other man, but somehow she knew he wasn't flexing for her on purpose. He wasn't the least bit vain. Poppy crawled back over his legs to settle herself across his muscular thighs, and wondered if he'd planned it this way—guiding her to be on top this first time, so she didn't feel overwhelmed by his size. It was exactly the kind of considerate thing BL might think of. He grabbed the little foil packets out of her hand, tossed two on her night table, and ripped the third open with his teeth. He obviously didn't want to remove both hands from her, probably to keep her from getting away.

After he'd covered himself, though, George paused and stared up at her. "You're sure about this?" he asked, solemn and painfully adorable.

Poppy didn't bother answering. Given her position, she thought her answer was completely clear. Instead, she lifted herself up on her knees, took George in her hand, and slid smoothly down over him until their bodies were notched tight against each other. George's head slammed back into her pillow, and he groaned. Poppy could empathize. BL was not a small man by any measure, and it had been a while for her. The sensation of him filling her definitely required a moment of silent acknowledgement.

However, the longer she stayed still, the less able she was to move. As the seconds extended into a minute, and then into two, George became aware that she was frozen. And with his usual solicitousness, he moved one hand from her hip to reach up, push her hair back, and caress her cheek.

"Poppy? Are you all right?" he asked gently. And just like that, with the careful sound of his concern, the whole evening came back to her. The stress of trying to impress the iceberg that was Sarge, the knowledge that Mini was likely to screw her over not because *she* was inadequate, but because he was petty. And finally, the notion that this was no ordinary contractor lying beneath her, but in fact a suave, cultured British aristocrat that she had no business fooling around with. George was bound to realize that before long, but when he did it would be too late for her. It was *already* too late for her, and the thought of having to nurse a shattered heart on top of everything else was a crippling one. Poppy gasped in a ragged inhale of air, and shook her head. No. She was not okay.

George withdrew, then rolled them smoothly until he was stretched on top of her. Poppy was tucked beneath his big frame on all sides, safe and protected from anything the world might throw at her. Instead of being overwhelming, though, it felt incredibly comforting. A relief. His hands were gentle as he smoothed her hair back off her forehead. His lips were tender as he planted whisper-soft kisses on her forehead and nose and chin. George pulled back just far enough to study her face. Poppy relaxed. There was no anger, no frustration there in his expression. Nothing that spoke of their differences of birth or social status…only inquiry. She smiled. This man was a saint.

"How about now?" he asked her quietly.

"Much better," she agreed.

"Was that getting to be too much of a performance?" he murmured against her neck, nuzzling into the space below her ear. There was no demand in the gesture, just a genuine delight in all things Poppy. God, he was sweet. The rhythm of her heart settled, mirroring the steady beat of his, thumping reliably away in his chest.

"A little bit," she admitted in a whisper.

"Are we done?" he questioned. Poppy was sure he'd never penalize her if she said yes. But George also had some seductive tricks of his own up his sleeve. He undulated his hips against hers in a very, very fetching way. Oh, he was good. Poppy was back on track just like *that*.

"No!" she managed to gasp out. At George's throaty chuckle, she felt compelled to add, "Not done!"

George slid back into her then, more slowly than she'd done the deed, to be sure. He pulled back and did it again, and his motions changed the whole tenor of their interaction. In an instant, he had altered things from torrid banging to making love. Poppy had thought she needed the white-hot obliteration of the first, but she was wrong. And George knew it. There were advantages, it seemed, to hopping in the sack with a guy who could see right through you.

"Oh, God, Poppy," he murmured against her lips. "You're so beautiful."

Poppy felt herself blushing. How could one reticent man make her feel the truth of those words so easily? George was worshiping her with every stroke of his hands and motion of his body. He maintained a slow and steady pace as long as either of them could endure it. Poppy was a quivering mess, but she couldn't quite reach the spot she needed to get to. The tendons in George's neck were taut with the strain of his control.

"George, *please*," Poppy begged.

It seemed to be the permission he needed to let himself off his leash. He hooked his hands under her knees and pulled, wrapping her legs high around his waist. Then he braced himself on his forearms and began driving into her faster. Harder. Poppy suddenly understood that all those muscles had functions extending well beyond refinishing floors.

"Come on, love," George chanted in her ear. "Come on." He'd been keeping himself in check more than she realized. Poppy tightened her legs around him, grabbed onto his broad straining shoulders, and…flew. George arched his neck and froze in place, letting the sensation wash over him for long moments before finally collapsing beside her, breathing hard.

As they lay in her bed after, Poppy realized that her world had tilted on its axis somehow. That hadn't been any ordinary "shagging" as George might put it. But it was hard to say what it did mean. Poppy blinked in the darkness well into the night, trying to puzzle things out. For someone who clearly wasn't meant to be hers, this man beside her felt an awful lot like The One.

POPPY DIDN'T KICK him out after they did the deed. Instead, she let him lie in her bed next to her, tracing soft little circles on her

shoulder blade while her body went boneless and sleepy. George didn't know why, of all the possible times that the thought could occur to him, he was suddenly thinking about Charlie's smirking caveman comment. Exactly as his little brother had predicted, George had just hoisted Poppy over his shoulder and stalked off to have his way with her. He grinned mightily. It had worked rather well, too, if he did say so himself.

His grin turned into a chuckle, and from there, a full-blown belly laugh. Soon, his sides were aching and tears were streaming down his face. It felt like a year's worth of angst was flowing out of him, and George couldn't seem to stop. Poppy leaned up on his chest and stared down at him in confusion, which only made things worse. Dear God. He'd really lost his marbles this time. How was he supposed to explain?

He settled on, "I really needed that, sweetheart."

It seemed to work. She smiled back at him and agreed, "Me too."

THE NEXT MORNING, George awoke to discover Poppy already up. Her knees were bent, and she was trying to prop a heavy, unwieldy textbook against them. She had a tight, beat-up little t-shirt on, and her glasses perched on her nose. George had a hard enough time keeping his hands to himself when she was dressed and primped for the outside world. But if this was how she looked in bed first thing in the morning, he didn't have a prayer. She was frowning adorably, flipping quietly back and forth between the index and the center pages, looking for something. Without makeup, which she must have washed off sometime after he'd fallen asleep, he saw that she had faint tawny freckles across her nose. Her lips were a soft, deep rose color and looked like they'd been kissed half the night. Which they *had*, he congratulated himself.

But she also had blueish smudges under her eyes. And her shoulders were tense. She reached for the coffee on the table beside her, gulped it with jerky movements, then plunked the cup back down. Her hand scrabbled through the covers, searching. George plucked the large yellow highlighter up from where it dug into his thigh and placed it in her hand. Poppy's gaze flew to his, and he jerked in shock. Lord, she looked raw and vulnerable, not sated and oozing afterglow. This was bollocks. They still had one condom left to work with.

"Oh! Hey BL, I didn't realize you were awake." She looked from her book, to him, then back again.

George stretched his arm behind his head, then watched her eyes follow the movement and glaze slightly. He *might* have flexed his bicep for her. Just a tad. He inched up in the bed, and the covers slipped down his bare chest. Poppy noticed that, too, and started to look a little less anxious. George jerked his chin in the direction of the book. Best to give her a moment to warm up to the idea.

"What are you studying?"

"Uh…" she looked sheepish. "Last night—were you with me when Sarge mentioned that artwork they wanted to obtain? The one they were raising money for?"

George nodded. It had been an uncomfortable exchange. He'd had the distinct impression the woman had been trying to get a rise out of Poppy with the discussion. Poppy had played it cool, but underneath the façade, he'd felt her tension.

"That woman was all mouth and no trousers," he grumbled. "She probably has never seen it either."

"I'm trying to look it up. I've never even *heard* of it, and I thought I should learn more about it. Especially if that's going to be the big thing they're working on next year." With shaky hands, Poppy highlighted something on the page, then flipped back to the index. The book slid sideways, and George shot a hand out to catch it before it nailed him right in the family jewels.

"Sorry. God," she laughed nervously. "I should do this later." She glanced at her little alarm clock, trying to be discreet. "Do you want some coffee?"

George's hopes for a reprise of last night's activities were waning fast. "I would love some," he said. "Do you study like this a lot?" he inquired, taking in the angle of her knees. The size and weight of the book.

"Yeah. Pretty much," Poppy admitted. "Not enough hours in the day, you know?"

George nodded, thinking about the highlighter. "You need a lap desk," he told her. "Something you can prop the book on that will keep the weight off your legs."

Poppy thought about that, blinking rapidly. As pillow talk went, it probably wasn't the best. "Yeah," she agreed, "You're probably right." Poppy fished a pen out of the sloppy bun she had her hair in, capped the highlighter, and set them both aside on her night stand. "Something with a place for pens."

"I'll make you one," George told her. He could already see it in his mind. The way it would fold flat, so she could slip it between the night table and her bed, and she wouldn't trip over it during the day. The way it would rest over her lap. How he would sand the wood so smooth, it would never snag her clothes or bedding, or scratch that delicate skin of hers.

Poppy shrugged, looking a wee bit bewildered. "Uh, okay," she said. "But you don't have to."

"I know," George agreed. "I want to."

Poppy still did not have the lazy, languid, fucked-half-the-night look about her that he wanted her to have. That *he* probably had. She looked antsy, not sensual. Like she had places to be. Which, of course, she *did*, because she was busy as fuck. And he was an arse for lounging around keeping her from it.

"How about that java?" he asked, knowing he had to clear out now, despite it being virtually the last thing he wanted to do.

Poppy nodded, and leaped up. "Coming right up," she said, then fled.

Twenty minutes later, George was dressed in last night's tux and sitting behind the wheel of Edward's 5 series sedan, wondering what the hell had just happened.

Chapter Six

GEORGE SAT ON Edward's steps, fussing with his phone and waiting for his wayward brother to make his appearance. He knew Ed had been entertaining Meg the night before, and he hoped that had been the pivotal event they were all hoping for. If Edward had managed to not act like a right foul git, he might've gotten Meg in the sack with him. There was no way on God's green earth that wouldn't jog a man's memory—those two had been thick as thieves the whole of last autumn.

Once he'd gone home and showered, George had picked up some breakfast for the two of them, then headed over here to round up Ed. He hadn't wanted to wash the scent of Poppy's perfume from his skin, and he would rather be eating breakfast in bed with her than cooling his heels on the stoop of some Back Bay brownstone, but he'd been booted out unceremoniously. It was just as well. He and Ed *did* have an appointment, and it wouldn't do to skip out on it, even for some first-class shagging. It was best to just accept things gracefully.

George realized he was feeling uncharacteristically optimistic. For a lark, he downloaded the image of a big, blowsy red bloom, then made it the screen saver on his phone. Who would have guessed it? All these years they had been throwing tepid English roses his way, and as it happened, what he'd *really* wanted was a florid hothouse flower. Poppy—he knew, once the gears of her nimble brain had started turning again this morning, that something was off between them. But George found he couldn't quite work up any concern about it. She had to know, just as well as he did, that last night there had been nothing that could come between them. They were as perfect together as two people could be in those moments when they were wrapped in each other's arms.

It hadn't escaped George's attention last night that her panties had been little cotton leopard-print bikinis. Only Poppy, he thought, could be counted on to match her knickers to her shoes. He stilled for a moment, mind wandering back to that first morning in the chapel, when she'd been wearing hot pink combat boots. If his suspicion was correct, she might have been wearing bright pink skivvies then, too—knowing her, with some cheeky phrase screen-printed across them. Something like "Wednesday," even though it had been Monday. Or "Closed for Business." He grinned, then refocused on the moment at hand. How had he made it twenty-four years without realizing that someone like Poppy was exactly what he wanted and needed? Sass. Cheek. Unpredictability. And somehow, all that was mixed with stability, responsibility, and kind-heartedness in one extraordinary woman. It seemed impossible to believe. But there Poppy had been, lavishing him with affectionate open-mouthed kisses half the night. And George didn't think he'd ever want to let her go, whether she could really help him with Ed or not.

EDWARD, OF COURSE, had forgotten their appointment. He couldn't be counted on to remember the love of his life—how was he supposed to recall that they were meeting new clients this morning? When his brother stumbled out his front door, looking for all the world like he was planning to take a hungover run around the block, George knew. He'd blown it again, bolloxed things up with Meg, and once again George was going to have to find some way to patch things over.

Seriously, how much longer could this go on? George had been slapping thick layers of spackle over the holes in his brother's relationship every few days, but he couldn't possibly expect Meg to put up with it much longer. He'd seen the look on her face, and making her endure much more of this shit would be bloody cruel. He couldn't do it to her.

But Edward—damn it, Edward looked even more crestfallen than George presumed Meg felt. On top of that, he'd started spouting some rubbish about being in love with a woman who was not Meg last fall. *Christ.* All George could think to do was tuck some greasy food into him and get the man moving, focusing on work and not all the ways he was deficient. Hell, it worked for George, and they *were* brothers after all.

George wasn't entirely sure how it happened, but somehow, in the time it took for Ed to get showered and for them to get on the road to the appointment with the Wilkinsons, his brother had worked a conniving magic trick. Somehow, George had been put in the unenviable position of acting as intermediary between Edward and Meg. It wasn't like he *wanted* to do it, but he didn't see how he had a choice—not if he wanted Ed to get better. And he *really* did.

George had to go along with it. As yet, Poppy hadn't provided a single new or useful idea about how to get through to Edward, not that George blamed her. He was still convinced Meg might be the key to unlocking everything. And so, despite knowing that their shagfest had been a total debacle, he was going to keep throwing Edward and Meg together until they just wouldn't do it anymore.

George hadn't been able to get Edward to agree to anything romantic or one-on-one. Something about not wanting to give Meg the wrong idea? It was all shit, and Ed was acting like a temperamental, disagreeable little child. The best George had been able to manage was a group outing to watch a soccer match at the pub. Dinner and the theater, it was *not*—even George's mulishness had its limits.

The whole morning in Edward's company, coupled with that extremely uncomfortable call to Meggers, had pretty much wiped clean any lingering sense of joy left over from his night with Poppy. She'd been too booked up to meet with him again today, so when George got off work, he threw himself into making the lap desk for her. It was simple enough to construct, and the process of hammering and sanding and staining it made him feel closer to her somehow. As if he could pour his outsize feelings into an inanimate object and have it mean something bigger. It made George feel like he had something to offer Poppy, despite the fact that she was vibrant and smart and unique, and he was an unexciting, uncomplicated man who labored with his hands. His mind wandered, thinking of other things he might make her, assuming that she let him stick around. George refused to give up before he'd given it a real go, though. He was too far gone and too stubborn for that. He'd find some way to convince her that they were meant to be.

HE'D HAD TO fairly beg, but Poppy moved some things around so she could come to the pub with him. After all, if Meg could bring her whole support system with her, why couldn't George? He met Poppy at her apartment first, though, so he could present her with the desk. Charlie had been good enough to construct a beautiful box for it, and she seemed nonplussed to see George standing there at her door with it in his hands. Behind her, Nathan was snoring away like a degenerate on the couch. She shrugged, then beckoned George to follow her, so they tiptoed down the hall to her room.

Once Poppy opened the gift, George demonstrated how to extend the legs and adjust the angle of the book stand. He showed her the niches on the sides for her pens, and explained how to close it all up again. He wasn't sure what he'd expected, but Poppy didn't exactly throw herself into his arms in a great gush of gratitude. She seemed too overwhelmed for that. Instead, she marveled over his workmanship and thanked him repeatedly for his thoughtfulness. The whole exchange seemed terribly formal and stilted. George was left with the awkward sensation that he'd gone overboard and made a mistake—he'd given Poppy too extravagant a gift and somehow managed to put her off. Or perhaps Poppy merely hated it.

That unsettled and confused him. Didn't she understand that George would give her the world if he thought she needed it? He'd assumed, after they made love, that they were on the same page. The thought that maybe they weren't, that maybe Poppy didn't feel the same sense of inevitility that George did, hummed beneath his skin like an unpleasant electrical current.

Pretty much the last place he wanted to go was that pub, to babysit his big brother so the bloke didn't self-destruct even farther than he already had. George would rather be using the short time they had today to crawl into Poppy's bed with her, to take another opportunity to convince her she was his.

For the first time, George had to acknowledge that he felt a wee bit resentful. Edward hadn't really expressed *any* appreciation for a single thing George had done for him so far. Instead, he'd barged around acting like a testy little arse. So when they arrived at the pub to see Ed parked in a chair sullenly nursing his draft, George steamed right by the chap. He gave a perfunctory wave to Charlie and his crew, then marched Poppy off to a table at the very edge of the group. If she could only spare him an hour and a half today, George intended to make it count. And his brother could just go hang for all he cared.

Needless to say, gathering at a pub to watch soccer was a poor substitute for Edward and Meg going to the theater like they had planned. At this point, George would take what he could get, though. It was enough that he'd managed to get his own personal star-crossed lovers in the same room with each other again.

When Edward signaled from the bar asking if they wanted snacks, George gave him a thumbs-up. The more distraction they all had from the train wreck unfolding in front of them, the better. Based on his expression alone, Ed was in rare form, even for him.

"Sorry I can't stay long," Poppy reminded George. "I have a shift at Jazz in an hour." She'd colored her hair again. Now the black was streaked with hot pink and vivid red. She smelled brilliant, too, and had painted her lips a luscious, bite-able red.

"Just an hour?" George asked her, disappointed. "I thought we had longer."

"Sorry," Poppy replied, and she almost sounded like she really was. "Katie called in sick."

"It's okay," George told her. But it didn't feel okay. He was ten kinds of frustrated.

"I can't believe you made that desk without any plans," she tried. "It's really beautiful. Thank you."

Why did that irritate him so much? Whatever he'd been hoping to communicate to her with the gift had clearly missed its mark. "Well—I said I would...so I did," he blurted out. But now he just sounded like a prick.

Poppy's wounded tone only underlined the point. "It's really pretty, though," she murmured. "I'm touched that you thought of it."

"I put a topcoat on it," he explained. "So the stain wouldn't rub off on your bedding."

"Oh, okay," Poppy said, nodding.

"I know it smells a little strong, but that will go away soon. It's completely dry, though. Don't worry about that," George added. And...*why* was he telling her all this?

Poppy seemed to be wondering the same thing. "I wasn't even kind of worried, but thanks."

"And I showed you how it works? How to set up the book stand?" he mumbled distractedly, completely unable to rein in his own mouth.

"You sure did," Poppy drawled, exasperated. "Twice. It's not hard."

"I'm sorry, love, I don't mean to be an arse," George told her then. He tucked her under his arm and breathed in her steadying scent. "I'm just all cock-eyed with the way this shit is going with Edward."

George had herded her off to the side of the group when they arrived, so he could shield her from Charlie's smutty friends and Edward's foul mood, and hopefully talk to her a little. But now Poppy peered around his body, taking in the pub and the expression on his older brother's face.

"Oh, no. George, *no.* This is all wrong for them," she hissed.

"I know," he said grimly.

"Why here? This isn't romantic at all!" Poppy complained.

"Poppy, love, I *know.* I think that was the point. He would *not* agree to anything romantic. This was the best I could manage."

"Maybe I should talk to him. Maybe I can say something that will trigger a memory. I mean...*dude.* They used to come into Jazz every week looking for each other! How do you forget something like that?"

"Look, he's not in good shape right now. Let's hold off on you confronting him for a bit, okay sweetheart?" George asked. Even though what Poppy was offering was exactly what he thought he'd wanted from her.

She watched Edward for a moment. "Are you *sure* they really slept together?" she asked. George had let loose that little tidbit on the ride over here.

Right on cue, the front door of the pub swung open and Meg walked in with two friends. Poppy took one look at her face, then at Edward's, before swinging back toward George.

"*That* bad?!" she exclaimed, too loud.

He nodded, feeling appallingly morose as he got to his feet.

"How is that even possible?" Poppy demanded, incredulous.

"I have no fucking idea, sweetheart, but now that sex didn't work, I am shit out of ideas."

It all went downhill from there. Edward steadily ignored Meg and her companions, focusing on the telly with almost manic concentration. Meg grew increasingly affronted. Charles was no help at all, no big surprise there. And George couldn't even drink, because he'd promised to run Poppy over to work in an hour. Driving the Boston streets was enough of a headache on its own, without trying to add a DUI to the mix.

Too soon, it was time for Poppy to go. They slipped out the door and down the block to his truck. When he had them shut inside the cab, he leaned over, starving for a taste of her before he had to relinquish her again, but after a moment, George had to capitulate. That horrible scene back there in the pub had worked its poisonous sorcery—so that even kissing glorious Poppy felt weird and unnatural to him.

He tried again when they reached Jazz & Java, then attempted to arrange another date with his woman, but failed on both scores. Brilliant. George wanted to slink home with his tail between his legs, but even that was denied to him. He still had his dickhead brother to contend with. At least he knew the pub had decent scotch.

GEORGE DRANK TOO much scotch. They both did. It was the only explanation for why, when George tried to walk his brother home and Edward demanded to go see Meg instead, George agreed. Blimey, even a bloody moron could tell it was a bad idea. So why had George done it? The longer he sat on that chilly bench outside her building, feeling daft as a brush and waiting for Ed to come back out, the less he was able to answer that most basic question. Christ, Edward was likely to spout some crap about the mysterious other woman he'd concocted in his addled brain, and then what was Meg supposed to do? And where would that leave George? In the bloody shitter, that's where.

Sure enough, when George's brother eventually emerged from the front doors of the apartment building, George knew the idiot had taken a sledgehammer to any last remaining chance he'd had with Meg. It was all over. Ed would likely never see the woman they'd all expected to make family ever again.

George brought Edward home—what else could he do? He was too exhausted, too drained in his very soul, to go anywhere else. He'd crash on Edward's new couch, and then, in the morning, maybe he would be able to think of something else to try. The brownstone was quiet and dark. Edward was three sheets to the wind, and George didn't even bother trying to get him changed before pouring him into bed and heading back downstairs.

He'd had a security system installed while Ed was still in the hospital back in the UK. Once George had begun going through the business receipts and so forth, and had seen what kind of dough Edward dropped on things like that huge stone basin in his front parlor—George had deemed it necessary. But it meant that with the motion sensors on, he couldn't head back upstairs again to check on his older brother. Besides, from the look of things Edward hadn't bought much else since he'd been back in the States. Before, the brownstone had fairly throbbed with happy possibility—a future for Edward with a lovely wife and a pack of happy, playing kids. But now he was rattling around by himself like a bear with a sore head, in this empty too-big house. Grim, ill-tempered, and alone, like the beast in a fairy tale.

George stripped down to his boxer briefs. Even though he'd already had too much liquor, he padded barefoot into the galley kitchen, snagged a beer, and dropped onto the couch. As he drank, he stared into the darkness and thought. What else might help his brother? A bachelor living alone was hardly new. And all of them, in their down hours, did much the same thing. George huffed in irritation. Hell, if he were home, he'd be doing it right now. It couldn't be more simple, and Ed would have no grounds to complain that it was somehow a commentary on his amnesia.

George dug through his jeans on the floor, found his phone, and called up the website for a department store down on Park Street. He ordered the biggest, slickest flat screen telly that he could fit in his truck, conveniently on sale and cheap as chips. Then he texted Charlie to tell him that he'd pick him up first thing in the morning. They could grab up the telly, come back here and install it, and all before Ed was likely to even stumble out of bed. He knew Edward was going to be hung over like a *mother* in the morning, given the amount of liquor he'd consumed. George himself had never been able to sleep in, no matter how drunk he got or how little sleep he had. It was best to keep busy, power through the discomfort.

He drained the beer bottle and set it on the floor next to the couch. Today had mostly sucked, but at least now he'd accomplished *something* to help his brother. In the morning, he would call the cable company and get Ed signed up for a sports and movie package. True, Edward was likely to find a way to cock it all up again, but short of throwing something heavy at the telly…George paused. That was not out of the realm of possibility right now, but he shrugged. *If* it happened, he'd deal with it then.

George stretched out on the couch, pulled the blanket over himself, and relaxed into sleep, thinking of Poppy, and the regular riot they could have if only she would agree to see him more. He'd had a setback, that was all. It didn't have to mean the end of the world, for him or for Edward. It was a little like trying to force a square peg into a round hole, trying to get himself to believe it. Luckily, George was a fucking wizard with a hammer.

CHARLIE SKIPPED CLASS in order to help George the next morning. From the moment George picked up his brother from a street corner near his campus, to the moment he left him parallel parked outside of the department store, Charlie bitched about skipping class. He complained about his hangover, he complained about how long Ed was taking to remember things, he complained about George's truck being too high off the ground—the list was seemingly endless. The one thing he did not gripe about was the fact that George had requested his assistance. The call was made, and Charles showed up. It really was as simple as that, and George tried to remind himself of that fact while he wrestled the huge, unwieldy television box into his flatbed. He tried to remember it as Charlie groused some more on the drive back to Edward's brownstone. In the end, George limited himself to one healthy punch to Charlie's arm, rather than burying his fist in his whiny little brother's face. It didn't quite pack the satisfaction of, say, a black eye or a bloody nose, but it got the job done, and George was able to move on.

They got the box up the front stairs and through the house without much trouble. There was still no sign of Edward, and that was just as well—he could be an even worse crybaby than Charles. George sent his brother to bring the truck around to the driveway in the alley out back, while he brewed a pot of strong coffee. It was hubris enough to tackle the errand they'd just accomplished on empty stomachs—attempting to set up the flat screen telly without caffeine would be veering into the land of fantasy. Once his brother returned, George still didn't like the look on his face. So he sent Charles back down to fish his heavy canvas tool bag out of his truck. In addition to his drill, they would need to mark the anchor holes and so forth in order to hang the television on the wall, and Ed didn't appear to have much more than take-away menus in his kitchen drawers. George and Charlie unpacked the box together, then laid everything out, drank their coffee and bickered as quietly as they were able. Just a couple of lads, bringing their big brother into the current century, hopefully in time for the Sox game showing later that day.

By the time Ed finally made an appearance, they'd made some headway on the installation. Good thing, too, since one glance at the man's face was all it took to understand that the situation was grim. It wasn't clear whether Edward was having another one of his head-injury headaches or just a simple hangover throb. What *was* obvious, however, was that Edward had been thinking, and any fool these days knew that couldn't be good. They pointed their brother at the coffee pot, and kept watch. It didn't take long.

"What happened to my sheets?" Edward demanded from the kitchen. "The blue plaid flannel ones, that mum got me last year."

Well. That was unexpected. George and Charlie stared at each other, and then at their older brother. The bastard had just gone and remembered something, for the love of God, something from right in the middle of his dead zone. And while that was fascinating, it did not mean George wanted Charlie to keep pinching him on the leg, or to actually *mention* to Ed that they called it his "dead zone". George sat there, trying to handle Ed and guide him through his disordered thoughts as gently as possible. As Edward kept talking, George realized that he'd never really asked his brother why he thought there was another woman last fall, besides Meg. To George and Charlie, the *why* always began and ended with Edward's memory loss. But as Ed explained his reasoning, it soon became clear that he was working with a set of pieces from an entirely different puzzle than they were.

George and Charlie trailed upstairs after their brother, curious to finally discover more about what he was thinking. He showed them piles of clothes that were obviously Meg's. He tried to describe the fractured images his brain had been throwing at him. And while Charlie and George could easily see how those snippets fit into the bigger picture of the prior autumn, Edward had managed to concoct a completely different tableau. It had an odd sort of logic to it, as peculiar as it was. Which, George was coming to realize, made it even harder to convince Edward of what was actually true.

And then Ed pulled out the ring. *Christ*, an engagement ring, a huge sparkling diamond, nestled in its bed of jeweler's satin. His brother had been sitting on that bugger of a revelation for months now, without telling a soul. No wonder his head was fucked. George had known Edward was arse over teakettle for Meg, they all knew that. But this—this was something else altogether. This was forever—true love—and George *had* to find some way to fix it. If only Meg would pick up his calls.

Chapter Seven

PROFESSOR COOPER SUMMONED Poppy to his office by leaving a terse voicemail for her the night before. Once Poppy made her way to Mini's office the next day, however, she had already fielded one frustrating call from her father *and* had a spat about missing beer with Furby. Feeling like she ought to keep the streak going, she then called the inimitable Sarge from the sidewalk outside the Art History department. Poppy wanted to make sure she knew the status of her internship application before going into the meeting with her faculty advisor, and Ms. Sargent-Chaffee was only too happy to oblige. In faintly disapproving terms, Sarge informed Poppy that not only had she *not* received Mini's recommendation yet, but he had less than a week left to submit it. Her brisk tone suggested that even that might not be enough to salvage Poppy's hopes.

Poppy's heart was absolutely sick at the prospect. But then she remembered George bulldozing that docent at the contemporary art institute…and suddenly she had the confidence she needed to take the last couple steps up to Mini's office. He was waiting, and gestured her impatiently inside. Without preamble, Professor Cooper immediately began carping that he'd gotten three messages from students the day before, asking him questions about last week's lecture.

"If I'm not mistaken, fielding these types of inquiries is supposed to be *your* job," he told her. "Imagine my surprise to discover that you canceled one of the Friday TA sessions and are not, in fact, doing your job at all."

Poppy had understood, almost from the beginning, that Mini didn't want a simple teaching assistant so much as a lackey. She had also assumed that her own student status would give her a little leeway when it came to scheduling, but apparently not.

Still, she reasoned, "Professor Cooper, these students have not attended a single Friday night session all quarter. When something came up and I had to cancel one, I didn't think they would care. Besides, they can still come to the Tuesday morning sessions," she argued.

"So you admit that you cancelled it," he fumed.

"Well, yes," Poppy agreed. She wanted to be annoyed with Furby for dragging her out that night, but then she might not have met George. It was a draw.

"Despite the fact that some of the students work and have other classes that preclude them from attending a morning session," Mini complained. "I expect you to reschedule the missed session for another night this week."

Poppy stayed silent, hastily reviewing her work and class schedule in her head. She wasn't sure that what he was commanding was even possible. He glared at her for long moments. Finally, Mini slapped his palms down on his desk, then began to shuffle papers around without meeting her eye.

"I have a package waiting to be picked up at the campus bookstore. You'll be going that way at some point, won't you? They've put out a new edition of the class textbook," he informed her.

"I see," she replied. The new textbook had been released at least six months ago. She knew this because she had gotten questions about it from incoming students before the semester had even started.

"When you pick it up," Mini continued, "Why don't you just hang on to it. I'll need you to comb through it and catalog all the changes and updates. Once that's done, I'll have Susan send you my next few lectures so you can identify where they might need adjustments."

As Poppy continued to stare at him, she understood two things clearly. One, that she did *not* have time to do this wildly unnecessary task—two of her servers at Java had come down with mono, and Poppy knew she'd be picking up extra shifts for weeks to come. She was overworked at school as it was, and the "new" textbook would likely have been sent with a leaflet that already explained the changes.

Mini just ad-libbed most days in class, anyway. The notion that he had any sort of prepared lecture notes was preposterous, almost as much as the idea that he would take any of Poppy's suggestions into account. The second thing she understood was that she was being punished—asked to do something stupid, pointless, and vaguely inappropriate as a way to test her. And she was going to have to take it, because the ever-impeccable Claire Sargent-Chaffee was expecting something from this man *soon*. Poppy decided to launch a salvo of her own, even knowing the timing was terrible.

"By the way, I spoke to Ms. Sargent-Chaffee at the Gardner. She called this morning, wondering if you'd had a chance to send in your recommendation yet." That wasn't precisely true. Poppy had called Sarge to check on her application. And, if she kept pissing Mini off, he was going to sink the whole damn thing for her. *God*, Poppy wanted to get the job so badly. With a summer internship at the Gardner under her belt, she'd be in perfect position to apply for a full-time slot at the Museum of Fine Arts when she graduated.

Mini peered balefully at her. He was not amused. "Which recommendation is this again?"

"For my internship application," Poppy reminded him, though clearly he knew. "She said even a standard form letter would be okay." Both of them also realized *that* was not true at all.

"Oh. Right," he said flatly, not meeting her eye again. "I'll try to have a look at that later. Susan probably has it," he hedged coldly.

Susan was Cooper's harried secretary. As one overworked woman to another, Poppy absolutely hated giving her another thing to do. She had not, as yet, been able to cajole Susan with either fancy coffee or donuts, and every time she passed the tired woman, Poppy wracked her brain for another way to charm her. But, short of finding Susan a different job entirely, Poppy didn't know what else she could try.

"I'll check with her," Poppy agreed. Mini was already engrossed with something on his large computer screen—his research on Etruscan artifacts, no doubt. It was an overt signal that it was time to make herself scarce. He didn't react at all when she let herself out of the cluttered, too-warm office.

GEORGE SHOWED UP again, this time while she was closing up Jazz for the night. Poppy had realized that if she put him off too often, he had a way of appearing on his own. But usually by that point, she was so frazzled that she was thrilled to see him. He came bearing food, he drove her wherever she was heading, and he was gorgeous and sane, to boot. An unbeatable combination. As Poppy wiped down tables, she explained to George how Mini had showed up at her impromptu TA session that evening, trying to micromanage things for the first time that semester.

"But that's rubbish," he complained. "You don't get a dog and then bark yourself."

Poppy smirked, both at the colorful analogy and at his obvious indignation. "Dog is right," she muttered.

But George, predictably, shook his head in irritation. "Not even close," he disagreed. He pulled her into his strong embrace, and even though she'd been on her feet for more than twelve hours and was holding a spray bottle and a grubby sponge, she let him. Poppy knew she shouldn't rely too much on him. Just because he was wonderful and perfect and always made her feel better, that didn't mean BL felt the same about her. He could have anyone he wanted, and once he got sick of what a hot mess Poppy was, George Hughes would move on to greener pastures. And if she didn't protect herself now, she was going to be utterly wrecked when that day happened.

POPPY LOST THE Gardner internship. She found out days later, when she checked the museum's website and discovered the announcement on the homepage. Sarge had chosen two candidates Poppy had never met and didn't remember from the charity auction—a young woman from Tufts and another from Harvard. And even though she'd seen it coming—had anticipated it, really— Poppy was still heartbroken. Professor Cooper had dropped the ball, most likely on purpose. How could she ever forgive him?

At the next lecture, Poppy could barely look at Mini. He was testy and cold as he set up his projector, barely acknowledging her presence. The students trailed in, settling into their seats. And then Mini began speaking about the restoration of some painting no one in that room but him had ever heard of. Poppy knew for sure that it wasn't in the textbook, and as she scanned the faces in front of her, she saw that the students were as stunned and confused as she was. Hurriedly, she pulled out her cellphone, trying to record what she could of the lecture so she could try to help the kids later. There was no way in hell Poppy could have prepared them for this, though they couldn't possibly know that. How could you plan for crazy? And then—then Professor Cooper began passing out quiz sheets. Poppy jumped up, trying to get his attention, but he steadfastly ignored her.

She caught the frantic, furious looks the students were shooting her way. He hadn't warned her about this, so he must have had Susan make the copies for him. The students would almost certainly fail, Poppy realized, once she snagged a copy of the quiz and examined it. They would blame her, and so would Mini, even though he had set her up to begin with. Professor Cooper had not sent –and never would send—a glowing recommendation to the Gardner Museum, or to any other museum. For his own petty reasons, he had destroyed her chance for the one internship that could have made her career. Poppy worried about what he might say to her thesis committee when they met. Now that he had an ax to grind, how might Mini cripple her there?

Poppy noticed the tunnel vision first, the way the edges of the room went dark and crowded in, like the end of an old Looney Tunes cartoon. Her chest felt tight, and that familiar, unwelcome choking feeling set in. Poppy grabbed her phone off the table in front of her, then scrabbled on the floor for her bag and her jacket. She lurched up as a clammy sweat broke out across her forehead, and stumbled blindly for the side door of the lecture hall. The heavy door swung shut behind her, echoing in the empty corridor outside. Poppy looked around, but nothing seemed right. Twice a week or more, she was in this same hallway, but now everything looked weird, alien, and scary. Guessing desperately, she jogged toward the right, trying locked doors, finding only dim lighting and empty, eerie spaces. No exits. No stairwell. She slumped down on the floor, huddled against the wall and hugged her knees, hoping to keep the contents of her stomach in place. She couldn't breathe. Her heart knocked around erratically in her chest. Poppy supposed she might get through this eventually without dying, but she was going to *die* before that happened. And then she knew things were really, really bad, because suddenly she wasn't in her body anymore. Like a bat, Poppy was perched up in a corner near the ceiling, watching herself

shake and gasp and cry down there on the floor, like she was
watching a disturbing infomercial on late night TV.

Who knew how much time had passed when Poppy registered
the sound, like a cricket chirping there inside the hall. She could hear
it past the blood roaring in her ears, past her wheezing breath. Past
the sound of classroom doors opening and closing and many feet
walking down the hall in the opposite direction from where she sat.
She looked around and realized she was inhabiting her own skin
again, looking out of her own eyes, sitting in a semi-familiar corridor
around the corner from Mini's usual lecture hall. Her phone lay on
the floor next to her, emitting that sound, and she picked it up
curiously. The panic attack was subsiding. Poppy was going to live
through it, yet again.

The alarm sounding on her phone was supposed to remind her
that she'd picked up an extra shift at Jazz & Java today. There was
no way in hell she could actually work it, not in the state she was in.
But Poppy felt inordinately grateful for the prompt, since it
apparently was the catalyst she needed to claw her way out of the
spiral she'd been in. With shaking hands, she texted Katie, the other
manager, telling her that she was sick and couldn't come in. And
then Poppy shoved to her feet, trying to think. She'd need to get a
cab. All she could think about was getting home and crawling under
the covers. There was a lot she had to do, but most of it would have
to wait for one more day.

Once she staggered home and locked herself in her bedroom,
though, she realized that there was one thing that couldn't wait, not
another minute: George. Her life had just gotten to be too much.
She was a fool to think she could juggle a boyfriend on top of
everything else. Furby was a continuing, ever-present headache, and
Poppy would somehow have to find a way to work with Mini for
the last several weeks of the semester. She was going to have to tell
her parents she had no intention of coming home for the summer,
because she seriously could not face three months of Whitlock Auto

Parts and the Orlando club scene. And now, naturally, Missy and Jeff at Jazz & Java were down for the count with mono. It explained a lot about their relationship (something Poppy had suspected for a while), but it still meant she'd have to pick up extra shifts.

She knew what she had to do. BL had been fun while he lasted, but he was not for her, not long-term. He deserved better, and she needed to find a way to keep on keeping on, for just a little while longer. How the hell was she going to get a different advisor for next year? She hoped Mini would not be so cruel as to talk trash to the other professors, but at this point she wouldn't put anything past him. As unpleasant as the thought was, he still had the ability to keep her from getting *any* internship at all over the summer, not just the Gardner one.

George was a distraction. He was the only negotiable piece of this whole mess, and so he would have to go. Feeling like the world's biggest jerk, Poppy picked up her phone with a heavy heart, and made the call.

Chapter Eight

POPPY HAD DUMPED him. Dropped George like a bad habit, and that fucking *sucked*, for so, so many reasons. Forget about his own issues—how the hell was he supposed to get Meg and Ed back together now, when neither one of them was acting the way he expected them to? And *Mum*—dear Lord, his mum. Violet had gotten a taste of having a daughter back in the fall, during all those weeks when Edward and Meg were wild for each other. George wanted to return that to her, and he knew with a bone-deep certainty that she wanted it back with a vengeance. God knew nice girls weren't exactly thick on the ground these days, and if the countess turned her sights to George to assuage that ache of loss, well—they were all headed for the crapper. He hadn't even managed to hold on to Poppy for a month. Trying to replicate the magic he had with her would be impossible with anyone new.

George would've liked to just throw on an old t-shirt and walk over to the pub. Sit on a barstool, watch baseball, and act like getting tossed away meant nothing to him. He couldn't. Did Poppy really think she could end things over the phone? It was ridiculous. He'd been caring for so many people, and had been longing for someone to bloody look after him for once. George's string of one-nighters hadn't done the trick. He had wanted something warm and soft to hold at night, and the women were routinely disappointed to discover that underneath his brawn, he was not, in fact, an IRA soldier on the lam. Lately his thoughts had turned to getting himself a dog, but that would necessitate moving. George didn't think he'd have the time for that, not with all his evening research on traumatic brain injuries, and holding Ed's hand nearly every fucking day to keep him out of trouble. The very last thing George had required was another person to see to. But Poppy *needed* him right now, damn it, despite what she'd said. And by some strange, unforeseen alchemy, being needed by her, being able to actually *help* her, comforted him in return.

Poppy hadn't sounded right on the phone. He chewed on his lip, thinking. It wasn't just that she was upset, blathering on about everything going wrong, and how that meant she couldn't see him anymore. As if it made sense for him to abandon her, right when they needed each other the most. No, it had been more than that. She'd been getting out of breath as she talked. In fact, by the time she hung up, she'd begun sucking in huge gulps of air between sentences, just like she'd done the last time he'd seen her have a panic attack. And her thinking hadn't been Poppy's usual logical, matter-of-fact breakdown. She was all over the map. George grabbed his phone, dialing her right back. Of course she didn't pick up, but he left a message, knowing she'd listen to it if she was able.

"Hey, it's George. You sounded off when you called. I mean, more off than would be expected. Anyway. Can you drop me a quick text to let me know you're okay? I'm not trying to manipulate you, I'm just…worried."

He disconnected the call, then grabbed his remote and flipped channels when the ball game went to commercial. His voicemail for Poppy existed out in the world for a whole five minutes, while he surfed the cable sports channels. He drummed his fingers on the screen of his phone.

U ok, luv?

He typed out the text quickly, then sent it off before he could think twice about it.

Srsly– pls let me know ur ok

He lasted another five minutes before that one, his concern eating away at him. And then, ten minutes and one Red Sox triple-play later, he fired off another volley of texts, like the wanker he was:

Look I know something is wrong
I won't expect anything just let me come help u

George sat there, thinking. What was the worst-case scenario, here? It *wasn't* the idea that he would get there and she would have already moved on, hot and heavy in the sack with Philby, for instance, or some other artsy blighter from her classes. No, the worst thing would be if Poppy was in real trouble, if she needed him right now and he was sitting here on his couch scratching his sack and too proud to go check on her.

Fuck it, I'm coming over

The text was almost an afterthought. He already had his keys in his hand and was heading for his truck when he typed it. George couldn't shake the troubling sense that something was wrong, the nagging feeling pricking at the fine hairs on his neck. He was almost to her apartment, breaking traffic laws left and right, when his cell finally, mercifully dinged with an incoming message:

911– come now

And then, promptly, another, more troubling one:

I need help.

HER FLATMATE, NATHAN, was the one to answer the door. His hair stuck out on one side, but his clothes were slightly less disheveled than usual. He had clearly been studying in the living room. There were books and papers strewn all over the couch and coffee table. Soft strains of classical music drifted through the air, providing a bizarre, soothing counterpoint to George's edgy urgency.

"Hey, what's up," Philby said. But then, inexplicably, he didn't move aside to let George in. Instead, he stood there, filling the doorway like some kind of overgrown tree, preventing George from breaching the opening and getting to Poppy.

"Hey, mate," George said, measuring him. Philby was tall—taller than George—but it was a reedy kind of height, and George thought he could probably take him if he tried. It wouldn't be a pretty take-down. There would likely be gangly arms and legs flailing every which way. But he could do it. He shifted on his feet, flexing his hands in preparation.

Then, after long moments of studying George's face, Nathan spoke again. "You do this to her?" He jerked his chin in the direction of Poppy's room.

George's eyes flew to her bedroom door in alarm, but the door was closed and he couldn't hear a thing. There was no sign of Poppy. Presumably Nathan knew something George didn't, though. "No, mate. Wasn't me, it was that bloody professor of hers. I'm the white knight."

It wasn't the magic phrase the flatmate was looking for, apparently, because he still didn't budge. George added, "She texted me and asked me to come," just in case Nathan was looking for evidence of an explicit invitation. George held up his phone, like that would help. He was going completely mental.

There was a loud thump from the direction of Poppy's room. When Philby turned toward the sound, it gave George the opening he needed. He shoved the other man aside, and barreled straight for her door.

Knocking softly, he called, "Poppy, it's George. I'm here—can I come in?" He heard a soft sound from inside, but couldn't make out what she'd said. So he tried the knob, turning it slowly and easing the door open a crack. Philby watched him silently, looming at the end of the short hall and presumably ready to intervene if necessary. It made George feel a little better, knowing that Poppy had someone else looking out for her, in his own weirdly haphazard way.

Her room was dim—the miniblinds and colorful curtains blocked out most of the bright sunlight. There were two large textbooks standing on end on the floor—George assumed they had made the noise when they'd slid off the foot of her bed. It took him a minute to find Poppy herself, but when he did the sight hit him like a sledgehammer, square in the center of his chest. Even having witnessed one of her panic attacks before, he wasn't prepared, George realized. As bad as that one had seemed to him, this one was most certainly much, much worse. He sank down to his knees next to her, not wanting to frighten her but desperately needing to get closer.

"You…came," she wheezed out. She was more of a mess than he'd ever seen her, her hair falling down, her face tear-stained and pale, her makeup smudged around her eyes. She was quivering like a leaf, tucked in a ball on her rug. It broke George's heart.

"Of course I did, love," he assured her. "Straight away." He stretched out his palm, laying it on her shoulder. It seemed the safest place for the moment.

"But…" she gasped some more, "Dumped…you."

"True. What was that all about, anyway?" he inquired, trying to keep any hint of annoyance out of his tone. Mere curiosity, that was all, nothing to spook her further.

"Had...to do it...first," Poppy explained. "Before you...realized."

Oh, this ought to be good, he thought. "Realized what, love?" Poppy was curled up on the floor, almost half under her bed, but now she struggled to sit up. George moved to help, but she warded him off with one raised palm.

"*This*," she told him, gesturing around at the mess of her room and of herself. "All this. No one...should have to...deal with all this." Poppy struggled to get enough oxygen into her lungs. It pained him to watch. "But...especially not...*you*." She poked him in the arm. "Once you...realized—you would've been...gone." Her chest rose and fell, but the pattern was evening out, becoming more regular.

"And that would've been bad?" he confirmed, just to make sure he was tracking her.

"So, so bad," Poppy agreed. While she hadn't let him hold her yet, his presence and the process of talking to him seemed to be settling her. She swiped ineffectually at her hair, and under her eyes. If she was beginning to worry about how she looked, she was probably going to be fine, George thought.

"You actually thought I'd drop you just because you're busy and having a rough go of it, did you?" George smiled at her. He had always admired his parents, but when Ed and Meg had gotten together, that had been the real punch to George's gut. That had been the first time he'd realized that what he wanted so badly was actually possible for someone like him.

Poppy didn't smile back. She simply nodded, staring miserably at her toes.

"That wouldn't make me a very nice person," George mused. She just shrugged.

George didn't think he'd ever laid eyes on a more forlorn human being in his life. He leaned his back against the side of her bed and stretched out his legs. And then, tired of feeling useless, he held out his arms to her.

"Come here," he said. Miraculously, she did, climbing onto his lap and clinging to his chest with barely any hesitation at all. He settled his arms carefully around her, then lifted one hand to pull out the last remaining barrettes holding her hair in place.

"Let me ask you something, Poppy," he murmured quietly.

"Okay." Her voice was muffled and soft, her mouth pressed against his shirt.

"Does this help? This, right here, with me? Does it help you feel better, or am I making it all worse?" He thought he knew the answer, but it was probably best to be sure.

"Helps," she admitted, hiccupping a little.

"Because I love this, you know. Don't get me wrong—I hate to see you suffer—but this? These quiet moments, where I get to hold you in my lap and play with your hair? I *love* this. I would go through anything in order to have this with you. I would put up with any mess. And I would hold you like this anytime, anywhere. In churches, on trains, in markets...doesn't matter."

"I get scared, knowing that I need this, BL," Poppy admitted. "I feel like I should be able to do it myself."

"No one ever said you couldn't have help, Poppy, especially me. You're allowed to lean on people and you're allowed to give yourself a break sometimes," George said.

"How could you possibly *like* this?" she wept. She might not have been shaking anymore, but George's t-shirt was already soggy and beginning to stick to his chest.

"Because I like *you*, I suppose," he told her. "I like you more than I like pretty much anything else." George smiled, knowing the truth of it.

"God only knows why," she muttered.

"Why doesn't matter. Just go with it, love." George pressed a kiss to the top of her head, and Poppy clutched him tighter.

There was a knock on her door, and Poppy's head snapped up, clocking George painfully under the chin.

"Yeah?" she called.

"Hey man, you guys, uh…you doing all right in there?" Nathan's anxious voice asked.

"Just peachy, Nate, thanks," Poppy answered loudly, her voice firm and strong. She tucked her head back under George's now-throbbing chin.

There was a long pause. "Okay. I'm taking off for a few. Catch you later, all right?"

George felt a rush of affection for the tosser, as annoying as he was. The guy obviously meant well.

"Thanks, mate," George said. They heard his steps move down the hall, and then the front door closed with a bang. Poppy turned to face George on his lap.

"Do you still want to break up with me?" he asked her, hoping against hope that she'd take it all back.

She shook her head. "I didn't want to. I just felt like I should."

"You shouldn't," he whispered. She *couldn't*.

"Well, I know that *now*," Poppy huffed.

"Does that mean I can kiss you?" George asked. The crisis seemed to be past, and he'd never needed anything more.

"I wish you would," Poppy told him, and then, like the sun breaking free of storm clouds, her beautiful smile finally broke across her face. Thank God. George kissed her, and then, when she so obviously enjoyed that, he kissed her some more.

LATER THAT WEEK, with matters resolved between him and Poppy, George felt ready to take another swing at the problem of Edward. After a semi-heated consultation, George and Charlie decided to take Edward to a nightclub on Lansdowne Street the following weekend. Not letting him fester alone in his house had been Poppy's idea, but it was a sound one. If he was going to insist on screwing things up with Meg, Edward ought to know what he was giving her up for, and why she had seemed like such a good catch to begin with. Poppy would finish her shift at Jazz & Java, then meet them there. George wanted her to get to know Charlie, at least—he had a feeling that the two of them would hit it off like gangbusters given half a chance.

On the appointed day, Poppy finished up at work and grabbed a cab, capitulating when George had insisted she not walk or take the T at that hour of the night. She texted him to let him know once she was waiting outside, stuck in the line to get into the club. He went out to meet her, leaving Charlie to linger at the bar making eyes at the bartender. Edward stalked away to make the rounds of the interior, looking ready to bite someone's head off. At least George wouldn't have to worry about his brother meeting anyone new—Ed was magnificently unapproachable in his current state.

Outside, George spotted Poppy immediately—she seemed like a magnificent tropical bird amongst the sea of black-clad crows lining the sidewalk. She was wearing a burgundy-colored motorcycle jacket, a silver belt, and black pants rolled at the ankles. A quick review showed her usual black-framed glasses and hair pinned up in the back. When she turned her head, he noticed that the red and pink streaks in her hair were now back to a soft turquoise color. With a quick glance, George checked the date on his watch and grinned. Yeah. Right on schedule.

Poppy raised one pale hand to her head, touching her hair in an uncharacteristically self-conscious motion. George noticed the silver rings on her fingers, taking up more than half the real estate—flat wide bands, woven ones with tiny rhinestones, and thin little rings that sat halfway down, not even clearing her knuckles. He had the strangest impulse to slip those rings off one by one and suck on her soft, sweet fingers. Just then, she noticed him.

"Hey, sailor," she grinned, dimpling up at him with her best coy come-on. His heart seized. God. Those dimples would be the bloody death of him. They were like his own personal Kryptonite. He was so, so relieved their breakup hadn't stuck longer than an hour or so. He would've been a ruined man.

"Hey, pretty girl," George told her, slipping an arm around her waist as Poppy shuffled forward with the queue. He gave her a pointed perusal, then kissed her cheek. "Looking good, hot stuff." She was wearing chunky black lace-up wingtip shoes, with rubber-treaded soles thicker than some of his work boots. For some reason that tickled him—Poppy always looked like she could walk through whatever messy crap the city might throw at her, even though he knew she was lovely and sensitive on the inside.

As she moved, though, her shoes caught his eye again. He realized that the uppers were coated in some kind of sparkling black glitter that flashed each time her shoes caught the light from the neon marquee. George thought she resembled nothing so much as a dark, dangerous fairy walking along beside him. He found himself hoping, irrepressibly, that the cute little toes inside those shoes would be painted with the same fire-engine-red polish as her fingernails. And how fucking crazy was that? Before Poppy, he hadn't considered the little flourishes of women for more than about five minutes, in all his time on earth.

"How was work?" he asked, mainly for an excuse to lean in and smell her neck. His favorite smell in the world. George knew—this was it for him. This woman, in all her messy, colorful, complicated glory, was *it*. She'd ruined him for every other woman, ever.

Whatever happened with Edward, either tonight inside this club, or out in the world every day after this, George was going to take this one thing for himself. He couldn't stop living just because his brother had, and he wouldn't—not anymore. Poppy was his future, and he was going to hold on to her with both hands. Whatever else life decided to throw at George, he was going to be facing it with her in his corner. And what a welcome revelation that was. He was freaking sick to death of managing it all alone.

Chapter Nine

POPPY HAD KNOWN that staying with George and letting the relationship play out naturally would come with strings attached, though at the time she hadn't been able to make herself care. Now, she had to wonder what she'd been thinking. His biggest condition had turned out to be an insistence that she go to a doctor about her panic attacks. So Poppy had dutifully scheduled an appointment with BU's student health office, and here she was, *waiting*. Not very patiently, either—the gripping urge to flee had her tapping her feet and wishing that she had arranged this for later in the week. Or next year, perhaps.

George was supposed to meet her here but had texted that he was delayed at work. He still hadn't shown up by the time the nurse called her name, and Poppy knew he'd beat himself up over it. At the moment, she had bigger worries—they weighed her, took her vitals, and sat her on the exam table with her feet dangling over the side like a little kid. She told the nurse her story, and a short time later, she told the doctor. It didn't take long before they were ushering her back out the door to the waiting room, holding a slip of paper with a referral to a therapist who could treat her more effectively. Poppy wasn't thrilled. On some level, she realized she'd been hoping for a simple, one-visit fix.

By then, George had arrived, dwarfing the orange molded plastic chair. He had one thick arm draped across the back of the seat next to him, knees sprawled wide, thighs strong and boots scuffed. He wasn't looking at his phone, like the other occupants of the waiting room, or even flipping through a battered Sports Illustrated. He merely sat there, taking up an outsize amount of space while staring at the door, waiting for her to emerge. The whole thing had taken no more than twenty minutes. He sprang to his feet when Poppy came out.

"Sorry I was late," he murmured, taking her arm and steering her toward the exit. "Mikey had to take off early."

At Poppy's questioning look, he elaborated, "My electrician. How'd we do?"

She held up the slip of paper with the name on it. "They gave me this."

George peered down at the name and nodded, "Cognitive behavior therapy. I read about that. All right. We'll make sure that he's the best guy before we commit to him."

"Okay," Poppy agreed. He kept saying *we*, she'd noticed, which seemed awfully nice of him.

"And I'll take the day off next time, so I can bring you," George added.

"You don't have to do that," Poppy told him. Just because she'd decided to stay with him, didn't mean she had to make the poor guy suffer more than absolutely necessary.

"Yes, I do," he countered, brooking no argument. "It was my idea. I'm not going to make you do it alone." And there you had it: reason number eight million why George was the world's best boyfriend. Poppy slipped an arm around his waist and allowed the gratitude to wash through her, leaving no guilt behind.

POPPY ENDED UP picking a different doctor than the one school had recommended—a woman who leaned more toward meditation and exercise as coping strategies, instead of relying so heavily on pharmaceuticals. Poppy and George had researched the side effects of the drugs the first guy advocated, and neither of them was too excited by what they found. Instead, George had helped her find Dr. Strauss, then sat holding her hand through the appointment while the new therapist told her to exercise more, to eat better, and to sleep longer. They'd work on Poppy's meditation skills a little more each week.

George offered her the use of his exercise equipment whenever she wanted, after Poppy admitted that she was intimidated by the campus gym. He even gave her a key to his apartment and made her promise to use it. Poppy discovered that, for a man with such a lily-white pedigree, George was not above blackmail. Not that she was complaining—he'd left her with a hickey on her hip that she'd gotten to admire for *days*.

It wasn't long before Poppy found herself at George's—only three days later. They'd met at a club the night before, where George had mostly ignored his brothers and paid special attention to Poppy in all the dark corners he could find. While that was all well and good, it was probably also good that George had made her go see someone, because even Poppy had to acknowledge that the attacks were beginning to come closer together. As it turned out, pretending it wasn't happening was *not* an effective strategy. At the first sign that she was losing her grip and starting to breathe funny, Poppy cut her morning lecture, texted in sick to work, and hightailed it home to change her clothes. She found a cab near the front of her building, and minutes later she was walking down the steps to George's basement pad and unlocking his heavy wood door.

It was weird being there without him. Poppy walked slowly around, feeling her heart beating too fast, and no longer sure if it was from the impending panic, or from something else. Something...George-related. She glanced at the spotless little kitchenette, and the perfectly made bed in his bedroom. Poppy had never been in the second bedroom, but found that it contained his treadmill and free weights on one side of the room. The other side seemed to be devoted to two tables full of woodworking tools and projects. Poppy drifted over, feeling a little voyeuristic as she examined what he was working on. She was trying to picture him building her lap desk—and enjoying the resultant image immensely—when her eyes fell on the second table. Propped in the center stood the unfinished wood frame of a little house—just the edges of the four walls, and the steep peaked roof. Poppy touched the wood with one shaking finger, noticing as she looked closer that the whole roof was on tiny brass hinges, so that it could be opened at the top like a box. While that was unusual, it was the intricate carving on each wooden spine that truly took her breath away— leaves and vines and flowers rendered with impossible realism and accuracy. Poppy had never seen anything so spectacular in all her hours wandering museums. George, her George—who thought of himself as some kind of brawny, lunk-headed laborer—had created it, and the notion rocked her to her shoes.

George was no ordinary woodworker. He was an extraordinary artisan, and he had *no* idea. Blinking fast and pressing a hand to her heaving chest, Poppy forced herself to step away, afraid of doing something to damage the fragile-looking structure. She stepped onto his treadmill, cued up a steady, low-impact program, and began walking. Eventually, as she studied that small house and all the bits and pieces of George's life strewn about the room, her legs found a rhythm, and her lungs did, too. Her heart was still beating fast, but it was a strong, regular drumming, nothing scary. Poppy felt secure in her skin, safe in this room, and hopeful that she could handle her life for the first time in months. And she had BL to thank for that.

Forty-five minutes, later Poppy got off the treadmill, and she had to admit she felt much better. Tired and out of shape, but better. Thirsty, she wandered into George's kitchen to see if he had a bottle of water in his fridge. There was water in there all right, and that wasn't all. The dude had maybe the best-stocked fridge she'd seen in recent memory. Meat, fish, eggs, a ton of fresh produce…it was like an advertisement for healthy, well-balanced eating. What bachelor ate like that? There didn't seem to be a frozen burrito in sight.

Rabidly curious, Poppy began peeking into cabinets, discovering that he was also in possession of a very nice collection of pots and pans, and a useful assortment of cooking utensils. Standing there processing *that*, Poppy suddenly knew how she could repay him for all he'd done for her. There were a select few dishes that she'd cooked often enough in her life that she could make them by heart—she was more of a recipe-following kind of girl. But Poppy considered herself a decent enough cook, and knew that George had the fixings for, at minimum, a pot of chili in his fridge. She also thought she could whip up a breakfast casserole for him. Her mother had made the same one for the Whitlocks every Christmas morning that Poppy had been alive. She could cook *that* thing with her eyes closed. George might be unique in a lot of other ways, but Poppy knew that, like most red-blooded males, he would love a couple of home-cooked meals. And since she'd already cleared her afternoon, Poppy had the time to make them.

Filled with resolve and purpose, which helpfully also wiped out every last vestige of the panic attack she had felt looming earlier, Poppy pulled out a soup pot and a large skillet, and got to chopping. First the onions and green peppers, then the cheese and sausage. The ground beef was browned, the vegetables sautéed, and the oven preheated. She was on a mission, determined to leave the food as presents for George to find when he came home at the end of the day.

She'd be long gone by then, of course. He might have invited her to use his gym equipment, but that didn't mean he wanted her camping out at his place all day, rooting through his stuff and abusing her key privileges. She'd *have* to leave eventually.

THE CHILI WAS simmering on a back burner, and the casserole was in the oven when George waltzed in at eleven a.m. sharp. It was basically six hours earlier than she'd planned for, and Poppy suspected she looked like something the cat dragged in. George had a friend with him, too, though she barely registered that detail. Poppy was too fixated on George's beat-up leather tool belt, and the way it hung low and sexy on his hips. The men hadn't noticed her standing in the kitchen doorway. They were too busy arguing about the Sox game from the night before, and about which place they ought to order pizza and subs from for lunch. Poppy had to clear her throat twice before she could get their attention.

George's eyes flew wide, and after giving her a once-over that apparently yielded acceptable information, he strode forward to plant an enthusiastic kiss on her lips.

"Hello, poppet. What are you doing here?" he asked, winding an arm around her waist and pulling her close. He was a little sweaty, a little dusty. He looked *gorgeous*. Poppy met the eyes of his friend over George's shoulder, and the man smiled faintly at her, taking a large, obvious sniff of the fragrant air.

"Catch ya later, you bastard," the guy said in a clipped Boston accent. "God, I hate you." George's front door closed with a bang behind him.

At the same time, George seemed to finally notice the scents emanating from his own kitchen.

"*What* is that smell?" he demanded, striding in there. Poppy had discovered a box of cornbread mix in his pantry, and had just pulled it out to make it when George walked in his door. He held up the box and waved it at her, somewhat accusingly.

She shrugged. "I, uh, wanted to thank you for everything. You know. I used your treadmill, so I made you some treats. I hope that was okay. You weren't, like, saving that stuff for anything special, were you?"

George's eyes grew rounder, and he turned back to peer into his oven, and then under the lid of the soup pot. When he returned to her side he stared down at her, then dropped to his knees in front of her and began kissing the toes of her sneakers like a supplicant.

"Oh my God, George! Stop! That's gross!" Poppy groaned.

"Who cares? I adore you. Truly," he said, chuckling and getting up again. "I can't believe you did this. Everything smells *great*. What is it? Is it chili?"

Poppy nodded. "And that's a breakfast casserole in the oven, with sausage and eggs and cheese."

George blinked. "Seriously?"

"Yes," she smiled, enjoying his bewilderment. She'd clearly found the right gesture. *The way to a man's heart*, indeed.

"When, uh…" George scratched the back of his neck, eyeing her up and down again, from her damp tank top to her black running tights. "When's it going to be ready?"

"Not long," Poppy replied, checking the clock on the oven. "You could probably eat the chili now, if you wanted. But the casserole has about twenty more minutes. I was going to make the cornbread, and then leave it all for you, for when you got home tonight."

"Interestingly, I'm home now," he commented. George was beginning to get a certain calculating look in his eye that made Poppy a bit nervous. "Twenty minutes, you said?"

"Who was that guy with you just now?" Poppy asked frantically. George was advancing on her in an alarming fashion. She backed toward the living room.

"Who, Phil? Friend of mine from the fire department. We bonded over a little electrical issue up on Beacon Hill last fall. The homeowner was very touchy and called out the hook-and-ladder truck for a bit of a burning smell—took Phil and me an hour and a half to talk her off the ledge," George explained. He tried to grab her, but Poppy danced out of his grasp. "But a beautiful friendship was born," he finished wryly. "He's going to be right pissed that he had to find his own lunch today."

"Poor Phil," Poppy tried. "There was plenty for him, too." George had backed her into a corner, and she looked wildly around for an exit. She was sweaty as hell right now. Unfortunately, unlike George, Poppy did not smell awesome when sweaty. He really should *not* be trying to get so close to her.

"Fuck Phil," George said with a huff. Then he lunged again, getting hold of her shirt and reeling Poppy in close. He dropped his head and nuzzled her neck, breathing deep.

"Mmm," he groaned, deep in his throat. "Did you set the oven timer, Poppy?"

"Well, yeah, but…"

"So it will shut off when it's done?"

"Presumably, but George—" she tried again.

"Come with me, young lady," he urged with a mischievous grin. He grabbed her hand and tugged her toward his bedroom. "I have something to show you."

Oh for the love of… "Is it your *hammer*?" she asked, rolling her eyes as she trailed semi-willingly after him.

"Screwdriver," he chuckled, tugging harder.

Poppy had to laugh. The man was freaking incorrigible.

But he was also on a mission, and seemed to be taking his twenty-minute deadline pretty seriously. George was out of his tool belt and steel-toed boots, as well as everything else he was wearing, in two seconds flat. Next thing Poppy knew, he had her wet and soapy under the hot spray of his shower, pressed between the bulk of his body and the slick tile wall. And really, there was absolutely nothing to protest about that.

True to his word, he had her dried off and back in a clean t-shirt of his at almost the exact moment the oven began beeping. She didn't think she'd ever been given such an efficient orgasm in her life. But again, she wasn't complaining—Poppy had also gotten a rain check for more hijinks later. As they sat in his kitchen with bowls of chili and squares of fresh-baked cornbread, Poppy finally remembered.

"George. You didn't tell me you did woodworking," she said.

"Sure. I do that," he told her between heaping bites. "Among other things."

"Are you as good at those other things as you are at woodworking?"

"You tell me, dollface," he grinned.

"You're cheeky, you know that?" she inquired, fake-scowling at him.

He smiled smugly, then kept shoveling in his food. At least Poppy didn't have to wonder if he liked it. She doubted the chili would last him three days, if he kept inhaling it like that.

"Anyway, what I meant was—I saw that project you're working on in the room with the treadmill. It's seriously amazing, George," Poppy told him.

"Oh, the terrarium? Just a little something for my mum for Mother's Day. My dad said her dog keeps eating her orchids. I still have to figure out how I'm going to ship it to her, though. I kind of thought they'd be back in Boston by now." He grew somber at the reminder of everything his family had endured, trying to rehabilitate both a father and a son. Poppy knew how keenly he felt the pressure to fix everything for them all. Her heart ached for him.

"Is *that* what that is? I was wondering. But George, listen—do you have any conception how beautiful that thing is?"

George flushed and shrugged it off, studying his bowl like his life depended on it.

"I'm serious. That terrarium in there? That's a work of art, BL— one of the most exquisite things I've ever seen."

He snorted, then muttered, "That's rubbish. What do you know?" Poppy knew he was joking, but she wasn't about to give up.

"As it turns out, I know an awful lot about this particular subject, Mr. Fancy Pants."

Another disbelieving snort, but then Poppy caught him peeking up uncertainly at her from beneath his lashes. George cared, and he wanted to believe her. Not as confident as he seemed, apparently.

"How about you just take my word for it?" she asked softly.

George swallowed painfully, then nodded, still not quite meeting Poppy's eyes.

"Would you, uh… would you like one, too?" he murmured.

"Maybe someday," she smiled. "Your mom might like hers to be one of a kind for now."

"Okay," he agreed.

"George?" Poppy asked. "You know you don't have to do it all yourself, either, right?"

"What?" His eyes snapped to hers, searching.

"Your mom and dad will be okay. Your brothers will be okay. And Edward and Meg will work things out if they are meant to. You don't have to carry everyone else's burdens for them. Just like you told me: it's okay to step back and ask for help," Poppy said softly.

Just as quietly, George admitted, "Sometimes I feel like the blockhead in a family of rock stars."

Poppy had suspected as much. "You're not, though. What you do—preserving the past so that future generations can enjoy it— that has real value. And actually, it's exactly what I want to do with my life, too. So don't insult yourself, or me, by acting like it's worthless."

George picked up his piece of cornbread from his napkin, studied it, then put it back down. "Hey, Poppy?"

"Hmm?"

"Thanks. For everything. This was all quite brilliant to come home to," he said solemnly.

She smiled, feeling light and free. "You are very welcome, big guy."

BY THE TIME they left George's apartment, Poppy felt so good, so relaxed and content, that she realized there was no reason she couldn't work her scheduled shift at Jazz & Java. George dropped her off before heading back to his job site. She texted Missy, the server who'd agreed to fill in for her, from George's truck. The girl could probably use a little more time to get better anyway. Standing at the register picking out music for the lunch rush, Poppy was feeling more like herself than she had in ages.

But when she looked up from the counter, she was stunned to see George's brother stroll up the sidewalk outside the café, pause to peer in the big plate-glass window, and then hesitantly come inside, just as if her thoughts had conjured him. Edward Hughes himself waltzed right through the front door—the venerable big brother, whose saintly qualities George could not possibly extoll more often, and who was slowly driving George insane with worry. He stopped just inside the door to look around, curious and open. Like he'd never set foot in there before.

Poppy knew he'd lost his memory, of course. George had been torturing himself about it for as long as she'd known him, and right now, that chafed like nothing else. Forget about the fact that she still had a few more weeks left in the semester to deal with the faculty advisor from hell, or that the freshmen she was in charge of helping were a bunch of spoiled whiners. Forget that she couldn't hire decent waitstaff at Jazz & Java to save her life. Edward was standing there looking pleasant and vague, when his brother—his strong, steadfast, adoring brother—was tying himself in knots in his efforts to help him…it pissed Poppy off like nothing else could.

As Edward made his way to the counter, looking up and studying the chalkboard menu over her head, Poppy tried to be understanding. She tried to focus on what it would be like to not remember whole huge, critical parts of your life. Like the way Edward had sat across the room staring at the back of a pretty girl's head, weekend after weekend, and the way he'd always missed it when Meg peeked back over her shoulder at him. He'd forgotten the day that Meg had brushed past him and panicked when she finally looked him full in the face. And then, when Meg lingered in the ladies' room, Edward had made accidental, awkward eye contact with Poppy herself. Using her sternest teaching-assistant face, Poppy had jabbed her finger at him, and then pointed at Meg's table like a commanding general.

Edward wasn't always a total tool. Once Meg had resettled herself there, he'd picked up his stuff and marched over, charming the woman like his life depended on it. She hadn't stood a chance. And God bless them, but every time Poppy had seen the couple after that, with stars in their eyes and gobsmacked with love, she'd felt proud of herself—satisfied and smug that she, Poppy, had a hand in making the right thing happen.

Until it wasn't right anymore. Until they stopped coming in— and Poppy had tried to convince herself that they had just moved somewhere else. That became impossible when Meg rolled up in there earlier this spring, with a baby stroller and a tragic cloud clinging to her. Poppy knew even then that something serious had gone wrong. How could anyone take a look at Meg's face and think anything else? But then she'd met George and learned the truth. The baby was Meg's nephew, and Edward was a slate wiped clean. Even reintroducing the pair, even herding them into bed with each other, hadn't fixed things. Poppy was suddenly, inexplicably furious.

"*Ha*," she said to Edward, grinning evilly. "I knew it." She was goading him, even though George kept telling her not to. She wasn't going to be able to stop, though. Poppy was just so mad at this man for hurting BL, even if it wasn't Edward's fault.

Mr. Oblivious had been standing there a good long while, and Poppy was about to be slammed with the lunch rush when classes let out. She smacked her hand down on the counter.

"Sorry?" he inquired, perplexed and not seeming to recognize her. *Really? Like he didn't know she'd been dating his brother all this time?*

When he cleared his throat and opened his troublesome mouth to order, Poppy held up her hand. He was still obedient, it seemed—helpfully, he clammed right up. Poppy did not have the time or the patience for his crap right now.

"Don't bother saying a word," she told him. "I know exactly what you want." He paused, trying to process that information, but over his shoulder students were beginning to drift in. She didn't have much time left. "C'mon, dude, you know the drill," she prodded him. "Eight seventy-five."

Edward fell into line and paid her. Then, like clockwork, headed right for his old table. Poppy said a little prayer of thanks that no one else had been sitting there. It seemed like a good sign that he'd shown up at all—now she just had to watch him to see whether something spectacular happened. George would want to know *everything* later.

A massive revelation didn't seem to be in the cards, though. Edward looked content, but not on the verge of a breakthrough. Frustrated, she stomped over to his table and plunked his coffee down in front of him. And then, even knowing what she said was false, she blurted out something that was certain to startle him.

"By the way," Poppy drawled. "Your kid's really cute."

Edward's response, as expected, was immediate. "I don't have a kid," he protested, in his fancy little accent, so like George's. Technically, what he said was true, but at least Poppy had planted a seed for him to think about. A little something to chew on.

"Hmm," she replied, giving him a *look*. More people were arriving, and Jeff was getting flustered behind the register. Poppy had to get back in the game.

For the next half hour, she was rocking and rolling, doing her thing. Taking orders, restocking the food line, refilling the cup lids and the napkins and the little can full of stirrers. When she finally had a chance to check on Edward again, he was rising from his table, gaze trained on a girl across the room. A girl who was leaving Meg's old table, who bore a slight resemblance to Meg but was not, in fact, her. Like a fish on a hook, he trailed out of Jazz after her, his plate and cup forgotten on the table behind him. The look on his face was intense. Oh, Lord. Maybe something really *was* happening.

Poppy sent Jeff over to bus the table, then called out to Katie that she was taking a quick break. In the back, she dug her cell phone out of her backpack and texted George.

FYI—your bro Ed was just here. He looked weirder than usual. Maybe keep an eye on him today?

His response took a minute or two, but when it came, she felt better.

On it. And then, a second later: Thx, Luv

Okay. It was going to be okay. Poppy knew it in her soul, and was comforted by it. George was going to take care of everything, as he always did when the chips were down. It was what that amazing, incredible man did best.

Chapter Ten

GEORGE TUCKED POPPY'S hand in his as they ascended the wide stone steps of the Museum of Fine Arts. Edward had insisted that George take some time off work, so he had basically been spending his days either in bed with Poppy or gallivanting all over town with her. She was on her spring break, and other than her periodic shifts at Jazz & Java, George had his girl all to himself. Once the rest of his family descended on town that summer, he would have to share Poppy. But for now, all he had to worry about was where and how often he could snog her.

It would never cease to amaze him how life could turn on a dime. One moment, he was hammering and sanding and painting away in other people's homes while his father and brother were having a gander at some conference back in the UK. And the next moment, they were both in the hospital and he was left holding the family together. Holding a business together. Being a nurturer and caretaker, when prior to that, just days before, he'd been best suited to skirt chasing and manual labor.

The same could be said for George's love life. It had literally changed with the sudden, unbelievable opening line of a bad joke: *A man walks into a bar*. But instead of meeting a rabbi or a priest,

George had run smack into the love of his life. The timing had been beastly for both of them, mired as they were in exceedingly rough patches of their lives. And George supposed others might look at him in his Bruins cap and work boots, and Poppy in her pinup makeup and cute glasses, and see a mismatch. But to George's mind, they were utter perfection together. He was arse-over-elbow for Poppy, and saw no reason that would change anytime soon. He certainly wouldn't spend a minute missing the one-off shags with the procession of tarts he'd known before. On any number of levels, Poppy put all those women to shame.

As they paid for their tickets and strolled into the first gallery, George took a peek down at Poppy's face. She looked as serene and content as he'd ever seen her. He supposed that had a lot to do with the efficient little chap Brendan, at the Contemporary Art Institute—he'd come through in a big way with an ace internship for Poppy for the summer. She'd been relieved and thrilled, and once she began her work and learned of all the connections the CAI director had to the museum here, she'd be even more excited. The internship Poppy had *actually* landed would set her up to get her dream job at the MFA better than the Gardner ever would have. And with that problem sorted, Poppy's panic attacks had been gradually ebbing, too. George had her eating well and exercising with him, and she was getting cracking good at the whole meditation thing. Coming along splendidly on all fronts, really.

It didn't hurt that a few weeks ago, the wheel of fate had lurched forward on its axis rather spectacularly, and it was possibly the best turn of all. For reasons no one would ever understand, Edward had ambled into Poppy's café one day all on his own, after months and months of memory loss and general foul moods. Poppy had worked herself into a right temper over it, and despite George's explicit request to the contrary, had prodded at his brother as only she could.

Naturally, she took credit for what happened next. George spent a nail-biting thirty-six hours trying to flush Ed from hiding while his brother was busily remembering his life from the prior autumn. Remembering small things, like his personality, and momentous things, too—like the soul-deep love he'd fallen into with Meg. As much of a hash as Edward had made of things up till that point, he did manage to right his ship just as smartly. When George had finally gone to physically roust Edward from his lair, George discovered that his brother was well again—that Ed had reclaimed his life and his woman, and George could now go forth and live his own life without guilt or regret.

In order to do that, George knew that the main thing he needed was Poppy. Poppy needed him, too, though she could still be reluctant to admit it. But having even a few minutes together could fix whatever botch job of a day either of them might cook up. And being able to sleep together at night, to wake up and drink coffee together the next morning, had become one of life's most blinding joys for George. Aside from the shagging, that is. His realization that Poppy often matched her knickers to her shoes, of all possible female quirks, had regularly made it impossible for George to keep his hands to himself. There he'd be, staring at a pair of fire-engine-red heels on her feet in the middle of some market…and then his brain would short out with images of the crimson lingerie sure to be lurking underneath her clothes. It was brutal.

Regardless, George had started toying with an idea. A small, unformed idea that rapidly turned into a full-fledged plan when he heard what Poppy's situation was soon going to be. As they walked through the exhibits, Poppy explained that her flatmate was suddenly, inexplicably graduating that spring. Which meant Philby would be moving back to Colorado, and leaving her with nowhere to live come summer.

George, who was getting to be quite the fixer of problems, knew of just the right place for her to move. And over lunch in the glass-enclosed courtyard of the museum, he told her all about it: Beacon Hill, very pretty, tons of space, reasonable rent, available shortly. Poppy, as expected, seemed dubious, but that was only because George had left out a *few* key details. No matter—she'd learn those soon enough. Helpfully, he offered to ring up his realtor and, wonder of wonders, they were able to see it right that afternoon. Who would have guessed it? His clever little bird clearly smelled a scam in the offing, but George had confidence. The only thing he *wasn't* sure of, was what he would do if she turned him down flat. If he'd totally misread her, then what?

POPPY SIPPED AT her glass of Prosecco and soaked up the atmosphere of the MFA's courtyard café. She couldn't conceive of a better day. In the last week, she'd accepted a ridiculously awesome *paying* internship at the CAI, thank you George. The Gardner may have gotten *Assumption bleu et vert*—a tiny 7x7-inch oil painting as it turned out, with a lurid history and a high price tag—but they hadn't gotten her.

Poppy had also learned from the department head that her request for a change in advisor for the coming school year had been approved. And what was even better? They'd assigned her to Professor Paloma Montes—the avant-garde sculptor with bright red lips and sleek black hair, pulled into severe ponytails that hung far down her back. Poppy had been too busy working up a full-blown girl crush on the woman to even think of a nickname for her yet. And that was before Professor Montes mentioned her friendship with Kiki Bartucci, centerpiece of Poppy's graduate thesis. It seemed like a dream.

Poppy was becoming a total rock star at managing her panic attacks, too. Though, thankfully, those mostly seemed to be going away for now. Poppy wasn't worried. If they came back someday, at least she now had some ways to cope that didn't include denial and wishful thinking. And if George stuck around like she expected him to, he would be there to help as well.

That meant that Poppy's only current problem was finding a new place to live come summer. She couldn't say she would miss Furby *or* his buddies, but Poppy was a little concerned about jumping from the frying pan into the fire with a new roommate. George had spent the last hour talking up some guy he knew who was going to need a renter, but the whole deal sounded pretty suspect to her. It wasn't that she thought George would knowingly hook her up with some dirtbag...she just didn't think guys had the same standards as chicks. After the last year living with Nathan Philby, Poppy had some definite requirements she was going to be insisting on. Like no drinking her beer, and no dirty dishes hanging around for days.

George's cell buzzed while they were finishing up lunch—his realtor was calling back to let them know they could see George's mysterious unicorn apartment in an hour. Poppy rolled her eyes but went along with it. George wouldn't let anything bad happen, and it wasn't like he or his realtor could force her to sign anything on the spot. Poppy supposed it wouldn't hurt to just look at it—her morning was crowded with art and George, she had a full belly and a glass of Prosecco under her belt, and Poppy was feeling relaxed about things. Easy-going, even.

Except, once they pulled up to the place, it became clear that it wasn't an apartment—or even a condo. In fact, it was a full-blown hundred-year-old brownstone on par with his brother Edward's house. Ivy climbing up the front, glossy black shutters, a quiet leafy street, cobblestones set into the pavement...Poppy couldn't afford a joint like this with *three* roommates, let alone one. Suddenly, the mystical dude seeking a renter morphed in Poppy's mind from someone like George's friend Phil, to a lecherous old perv looking for some young co-ed nookie. *Eww.*

Ten minutes in the door, though, and George's realtor indirectly allayed her concerns. There was no creepy old man. There was only a guy named Jim, trying to sell the house to her *boyfriend*. Sell it. As in, you got a mortgage and came up with a down payment and then you got to live there. Poppy ought to have guessed that the "nice chap looking for a flatmate" was George, but she'd been so blissed out from wandering the museum with BL that she'd been distracted. Ever since the chili incident, he would stop at nothing to get her to cook for him, and this just took the cake. Good grief.

The current owners had obviously spent all their money keeping up the outside. Because the inside of this joint—*hoo-boy*, talk about your fixer-upper. The place was a wreck. The walls were littered with smudges and nail holes, and some odd, bigger holes crumbling at the edges. The wood floors were scratched, the finish worn away at nearly every threshold. Wires protruded from ceilings and walls, dangling in thick black cords wherever light fixtures used to be. And the kitchen and bathrooms were travesties left over from too many decades ago—too new to have any retro cachet, but too old to be serviceable.

George had been dragged upstairs by Jim, to discuss things like wood flooring that had been sanded and refinished about ten too many times. Cracked tile, plumbing issues—things that would make Poppy walk away fast and that George was probably eating up with a spoon. After a cursory glance at the second-floor family areas, and the huge bedrooms on the third and fourth floors, she figured she had better leave the guys to their discussion. It wasn't like she could contribute anything meaningful—the most she'd said had been an occasional *holy moley*.

Poppy took in the calm all around her. The quiet and serenity of the house. She looked at the framework of the place and envisioned George's hands on it. His soul and his hard work filling the space. And Poppy herself was filled with longing. She knew him just well enough by now—knew how he made her feel when she was with him—to imagine what living here with George would be like. No question—it would be heaven.

Wandering down the stairs, Poppy paused in the front hall, looking around. The house had a nice, warm, cozy feel to it. She tried to pinpoint why. Soft sunshine slanted in the front windows. All the angles seemed right, and each room flowed into the next in an orderly, relaxing way. The air itself…just felt happy. Content. She tried to imagine what George would do once he got his big strong mitts on the place. Somehow, he'd find a way to make it even better. Of that, Poppy had no doubt.

As she pivoted, an odd light from the back of the house caught her eye. She drifted toward it, the dim hallway giving way to the little kitchen, then a sitting or eating area, and…incongruously, a small conservatory growing off the back of the house like a little jewel. The half-moon of the glass roof fanned out over the pentagonal space, the huge panes of the glass walls held together with thin black metal spines. Poppy walked over and looked out, trying to understand how the structure was supported when the driveway into the basement garage sloped down beneath it. It didn't seem architecturally possible, and yet—here it was. She marveled at how it seemed to have just sprouted out from the back wall of the house, gleaming, sunny…precious.

Poppy had no idea what kind of glass was used—it certainly looked normal enough, but it felt sturdy and strong when she pressed it with her fingers. Before she fell too far in love, she reminded herself that it would probably be frigid in the winter and sweltering in the summer. Someone had probably meant for it to hold a small bistro table and chairs, but Poppy knew that if it were hers, she'd put armchairs there instead. A cozy nook with an ottoman and a table for mugs…the image of her and George sitting there drinking coffee in the morning, while the snow drifted down all around them was a powerful one. So was the thought of drinking wine under the stars while they reviewed their days with each other.

George would play one of her old jazz records. Poppy would kick off her shoes.

As she stood there, one hand pressed to the glass, George walked up silently, met her gaze, and she knew he could see those things, too. *Wanted* them, too. "Renter," her ass. BL wanted a hell of a lot more than rent from her.

"I'll take it," George said to the realtor, who had walked up behind him. But he didn't take his eyes off Poppy's face.

"I see you've found my little surprise," Jim commented, superior and pompous.

George's eyes drifted over the frame of the addition. "Is it stable?" he inquired.

"Very. Top-of-the-line job. The seller is a chef in town. Had the area filled with pots of herbs, if you can believe it."

"How soon can we close?" George wanted to know. No discussion of money or haggling or home inspections. But then, that was George: no frills and straight to the point.

"I had one other thing I'd planned to show you," the realtor said, a slight note of irritation coloring his tone.

George took another look up and down the shady, leafy back alley, backed by a low brick wall covered in ivy. The red brick backs of the other homes stretched down the way on either side. No one else seemed to have an addition like this one. Barring onlookers loitering in the alley, their privacy seemed secure. Reluctantly, George grabbed Poppy's hand, then trailed after the realtor. She hated to break the spell, and thought maybe George did, too.

Jim the Realtor's final reveal turned out to be a workroom for George—a large, open, well-lit space in front of the garage bays, under the front stoop of the home. Large windows set high in the wall let in daylight on either side of the stairs. Poppy had to admit it was perfect for him. It even had its own entryway from the garage, so he could bring tools and equipment straight in without going through the house proper. He could open the windows for ventilation and, once he put in noise-proofing, would probably not even bother the neighbors.

"Yeah, so…I still want it," George commented, with barely a look around. "This will work fine down here."

"All right," the other man said. "Let's go back to my office and I'll pull some…"

"Jim." George's tone was terse. He wouldn't be going to any office. He still had a death grip on Poppy's hand.

"Yeah?" the realtor asked. For the first time, a touch of his Boston accent crept into his voice. He shifted in his loafers. Poppy suspected George was a tad different than his usual client.

"Make the call," George commanded.

Jim pulled a device from inside his blazer, then paused with the stylus poised over his tablet. "And how much will you be offering?" he inquired carefully. Based on how this was proceeding, Poppy suspected this was not the first conversation these two men had had about this. And that made her wonder exactly how long George had been planning this. She'd only mentioned Furby's moving plans that morning.

George smirked. "Just enough so they know I'm serious, but not so much they think they can take advantage."

"I see. And that amount would be?" The realtor wrote something with his stylus. Poppy thought it was probably something along the lines of "What the hell?"

"Jim, I kind of think that's what I pay you for," George remarked. In that moment, he sounded every inch the aristocrat, jeans and boots be damned.

"Right you are," Jim barked. Had it been Poppy, she might have snapped off a sarcastic salute, but of course, Jim didn't know George the way she did. He probably thought George would knock out his teeth if he tried something like that.

"Splendid. Now—may I have a moment with Miss Whitlock?" George asked him.

"Certainly. Why don't I just step outside and make some calls," Jim answered, heading out to the garage.

"Perfect," George said to the man's retreating back. Tugging on Poppy's hand, he urged, "Come on," then led her back upstairs.

"So? What do you think?" he asked her, once they had reached the glass alcove again.

"I think it's beautiful, but it seems like it needs a lot of work," she told him, trying to stay neutral, even though everything about his voice and posture made her think that something larger was afoot here.

"It does," George agreed. "Though it isn't as bad as Edward's place was. We'll need a really meticulous inspection to make sure I'm not missing anything."

Poppy didn't have much of a response to that, so she shrugged and said, "If you say so." He seemed to be expecting *something* from her, and that was about all she had.

George studied her face, holding her in place with his hands on her hips so she couldn't get away. "What do you think of the neighborhood?" he tried again.

"George. It's Beacon Hill. Everyone likes this neighborhood," Poppy retorted, getting annoyed. Where the hell was he going with all this?

"I don't care about *everyone*," he fired back. "I care about you."

"Oh, is that right?" Poppy demanded, working up a real lather now, though she wasn't exactly sure what about this was driving her so crazy. "Because you're looking for a renter? A *renter*, BL?"

George had crowded her up against the glass wall of the alcove, and now he caged her in with his forearms on either side of her head.

"I was trying to be humorous, you angry little tart. We both know I'm not looking for a goddamn renter," he growled at her.

Poppy knocked her forehead against his solid chest. "Then what do you want? Why the hell am I *here*, George?" She'd never been so exasperated in her life. Why in the world would this man drag her here, only to rub her nose in something she wouldn't—couldn't—have? Maybe George wanted her with him for now, but when the time came to consider forever, she doubted he'd be drafting her. And frankly, why were they having this conversation here, when Jim the Realtor was bound to come back at any moment?

"Sweetheart, you're here because *you* are what I want," George commented quietly. He ran his lips along the shell of her ear, but didn't do more. "You are the thing I didn't even know I was missing in life, and now that I've found you, I'd rather like to keep you close. Besides, you will be homeless shortly, and you deserve a real, peaceful, safe home to live in and complete your studies."

"My *studies?*" Poppy cried. "And what happens after? What happens once I graduate next year?"

George just shook his head. "I am making a total hash of this."

"You think?" Poppy asked.

He seemed unruffled by her tantrum. He just said, "Listen, sweetheart, I have a confession to make."

"Okay," Poppy told him. It wasn't like she was going anywhere. Not that she would—confessions from BL had a way of turning interesting.

"Remember when I told you how much I like you?" he inquired.

"Of course."

"Well, I don't. That was a lie," George said.

That stung. Poppy tried to mask how much it hurt, but doubted she was successful. Because George moved in quickly, gathering her tight against his big, warm, strong body.

"I don't just like you, darling. I *love* you. Madly. As in, you're the be-all, and end-all for me. I'm a total goner, ruined for any other woman. And I don't just want this place for me. I want it for us, and for everything I know we can become. But only if you want that, too," he declared.

Poppy gaped at him. "You…what?"

"You heard me," George declared. "Now how about telling me how you feel about that, instead of freaking out about my renter joke. For the love of God, I'm not fucking charging you rent to live here with me."

"George," Poppy stalled. "You don't even know if you'll get this place!"

"Let's just assume for the moment that I'll get it," he replied drily. "Do you love me or not, woman?"

Poppy snorted. "Are you shitting me? I mean, really, truly shitting me?"

"Not in the least," George said, and now it was becoming clear that he was at the end of his patience.

Poppy melted against him, all the fight going out of her. Sometimes her thoughts were so loud and jumbled in her head that she forgot to consider what George was thinking. He'd just declared himself to her in a big way, and she was being…an ass.

"Of course I love you, you big…" her throat choked on the word "oaf" as she looked up into his face. She refused to contribute to his own low opinion of himself. "Big, perfect man," Poppy finished. "Wasn't it *obvious*?"

"Not terribly," he muttered sullenly. "Hence the question."

"George, I'm crazy about you. You are so wonderful in so many ways that you don't even recognize, and you always know exactly what to say to me, how to handle me when I'm spazzing out, how to…" She'd been about to say *touch me*, but naturally, Jim took that moment to wander back up the stairs from the basement.

"Well, they must have been more eager to sell than I realized," he told them. "Looks like we have a deal."

George looked down at Poppy, grin spreading wide. "Yes, I believe we do," he agreed.

Maybe it was all the talk of the chef who used to live there, but Poppy realized her man was a bit like a chocolate soufflé: firm and able to withstand some heat on the outside, with a sweet, hot, molten inside that a woman wanted to dip into again and again. It wasn't a perfect analogy—Poppy had never seen George collapse under pressure, and doubted she ever would. But still she grinned at him, knowing she had the fixings for a brand-new nickname, though she had to wonder how he'd feel about being her dessert. Somehow, she didn't think he'd mind.

Poppy had already witnessed the way George would stand by his family or die trying. She knew that if he said he loved her, he would do the same for her, too. The poor soul had no idea what he was getting into, hitching himself to Poppy's crazy train. In fact, George looked so arrogantly victorious right now, one might think *he'd* been the one to win the lottery. As Jim the Realtor prattled on about escrows and signatures, George hooked one thick arm around her neck and kissed her, hard.

Poppy smiled at him and stepped back to take one more look around. She had a flash of what her life could be in the next few years, here with George. And that was definitely something to look forward to. Poppy had just made the deal of the century, in which she was going to come out the obvious winner. She supposed she owed it to him to love George back just as hard as she could, just as long as he'd have her. A deal was a deal, after all.

Epilogue

Four Years Later

POPPY GOT TO Violet's house late, and missed hearing Edward and Meg's big announcement. As soon as she walked in, George collared her in a bear hug and a lingering kiss, then pulled a small photo from Edward's fingers to show her.

"Get a load of this," he said, showing her the sonogram with two tiny pink bows.

Poppy winked at Meg. "Cooking up a hydra?" she asked, smiling.

"That's what I said," George agreed, nodding sagely.

Poppy gazed at him fondly. "Great minds think alike."

"For your information, it's two *babies*," Edward grouched. "*Two*." But then he glanced at his wife and smiled goofily. "Because we're just that good."

"Dude, stop," Poppy laughed. "But congratulations anyway. That's awesome, you guys."

George then showed her a piece of paper covered in sketches of baby furniture. "And Charlie thinks I ought to make all this for them."

Poppy snorted. "Piece of cake," she told him, giving him a squeeze. "You could do that in your sleep."

He tilted his head, studying the paper. "You think?"

"Sure," she agreed. "Slap an antique glaze on those puppies, and I'll paint all the trim."

"That could work," George mused, the wheels already turning in his head.

"Damn straight it could," Poppy crowed. As it turned out, their hobbies dovetailed nicely. George built all kinds of beautiful things from wood, and Poppy helped him paint it all. The extended family had been making out like bandits.

The countess stuck her head out of the hallway leading to the kitchen, looking uncharacteristically flustered and emotional.

"Poppy, is that you? Oh, there you are, darling." She appeared to be juggling a tray of champagne flutes, and George moved over to help her.

"Sorry I'm late," Poppy explained. "We're setting up the new exhibit, and the delivery truck showed up late."

"But I thought the Fitzwilliam flight landed yesterday," George's mother said, frowning mightily and looking like she might want to make a call or two. She had arranged for the loan of the pieces herself, after all.

"It did," Poppy assured her. "They just had to clear some stuff with customs."

"Ah. Brilliant," the countess replied, patting George on the back when he took the tray from her and began passing the flutes around.

Violet breezed over and enveloped Poppy in a fragrant hug, then stood back to examine her outfit. Poppy's hair was colored a rich, deep auburn at the moment, which her future mother-in-law assured her looked beautiful against her black turtleneck sweater, slim dark jeans, and leopard print flats.

"Oh! In all the excitement, I almost forgot!" Violet exclaimed, turning away.

Poppy glanced at George, who shrugged and shook his head.

"Alistair? Alistair!" the countess called. "Where in the world did I put that bag for Poppy?"

The earl came stumping down the hall, leaned his cane against the wall, then fished a small bag off the floor of the coat closet there.

"Right here, where you wouldn't forget it," he smiled, handing it to his wife.

George's mother handed the bag to Poppy with a triumphant expression on her face. "Go ahead, darling, open it!"

Poppy slipped out the tissue-wrapped bundle, then unwrapped what appeared to be an old concert t-shirt. Her eyebrows shot up and she stared at Violet and Alistair, standing side by side.

"You *wore* this?" she breathed in disbelief.

The countess clasped her hands together and sighed happily. "I told you I would find it," she boasted.

Alistair sighed too, grabbing his cane and throwing his arm around his wife. "That was a bloody good time, wasn't it?" he reminisced.

"Oh, Alistair," the countess giggled, "If we had gotten caught there, our families would have locked us up for a month."

"Or more," the earl commented grimly, planting a kiss on her head.

"Or more," she agreed. Then she turned to her assembled children. "Your father had to punch the lights out of some chap who was getting a little too rough with me."

A DANGEROUS GLEAM had entered their father's eye, one that George recognized. As sophisticated as the man was, he packed a brutal punch. George knew this, because the Earl of Westbroke had taken the time to make sure each of his sons could do the same. Edward, naturally, had made use of the skill in the most institutionally acceptable manner possible, by becoming a boxer for his army regiment. George's occasional fisticuffs, while probably less acceptable, were certainly just as effective. And Charles, bless him, had needed the talent most of all: first, when kids had teased him for being dumb, back before they'd realized he had dyslexia. That turned out to be excellent practice for later, when he'd come out as gay and periodically ran afoul of people who took exception to his orientation. God help the knucklehead who presumed Charlie was some lily-livered milksop, though—George's little brother could be as fierce as anyone when the situation called for it. As for Freddy, he apparently hadn't had much call to try out his left hook, not with three tough older brothers backing him. But the world was full of idiots, so one never knew. Speaking of things one didn't know…

George bumped Poppy with his shoulder, and with a stunned expression on her face, she held up the shirt his mother had given her, displaying the words, "Never Mind the Bollocks, Here's the Sex Pistols."

Edward, Meg and Charlie burst out laughing in utter disbelief.

"I think I like where this is going," George murmured, pulling Poppy into another strong hug.

"Unhand me," she squeaked, shooting a panicked look at his parents.

"Put that shirt on," he parried. "And I'll consider it."

"Maybe later," Poppy smiled, dimpling at him.

George raised her hand to his lips, planting a kiss right next to the diamond sparkling from her left finger and scorching her with his gaze.

"We've got plans later," he informed her. "Big plans." After four years, he could say that the living-together plan had been a wildly successful one. George adored having her close at hand all the time.

He would have married her six months into it, if she hadn't been so insistent on finishing her degree, and then finishing their house renovation, and finally, planning a wedding that fulfilled his mother's every unhinged fantasy.

"That's what she said," Charlie snickered, being an arse as usual.

Alistair and Violet raised their glasses. "A toast," his father intoned, "to Edward and Meg, and their expanding family." A chorus of agreement sounded from the room. "And to Charles, on his upcoming graduation," their mum continued, to raucous cheers. "And last, to George and Poppy, on their wedding." Just one more week and a handful of hours left, by George's count, until she was his forever, in front of God and country. "May your years together be long and filled with love," his mum finished.

"Here, here," his family called. George smiled down at Poppy, his beautiful, colorful, loyal little bride. Then he leaned down, stroked her soft cheek, and kissed the bleeding daylights out of her.

Lucky in Love

The Lost & Found Series

Kristen Casey

Chapter One

"I CAME OUT to my parents today," Sean said, leaning back in his chair and tipping up his bottle of beer.

Charlie turned immediately to stare at his friend, but the man didn't move his gaze from the television screen over the bar. That was big news, though.

"And? How did it go?" he inquired, not without some trepidation. The Callaghans were staunch Irish Catholics, born and bred in Boston's Southie neighborhood. They weren't what one might call open-minded.

Sean just shrugged.

"What's that supposed to mean?" Charlie demanded.

"Nothing."

"Nothing? Seriously?"

"Seriously. They said they, like, already knew."

That was perhaps the *more* concerning news. Given Sean's background, he'd been nothing if not careful. Careful not to leave any clues, careful not to be seen by anyone who knew his family.

"How is that even possible?" Charlie wanted to know.

"I have no idea. But honestly—they seemed relieved to have it out in the open," Sean told him.

"Well—that's good, I guess. How were they about it?"

"I dunno," Sean mumbled. "It was kind of anticlimactic. I was imagining this whole freaking scene, you know? But they just kind of sat there and accepted it."

Charlie watched the other man closely, but he didn't appear in danger of an imminent breakdown. "And how are *you* doing?" he tried.

Another shrug, another noncommittal noise. As if it was all no big thing. And yet—Sean had called, asking to meet. Despite it being the night of Charlie's graduation from university, despite his being out on the town with his whole family at the time, Charlie had dropped everything and come running. He expected he always would, where Sean was concerned.

They'd started out in the same freshman class at their design school six years ago. Sean had completed his program on schedule, and had spent the last two years working for one of Boston's preeminent advertising firms. Charlie had taken longer. What with his dyslexia, and that one semester he'd taken off because of his father and brother's car accident, he was only graduating now. However, his mum was firm about situations like this—it didn't matter how long the journey took, if you were right where you wanted to be at the end of it. Charlie was inclined to agree. Through all of it, though, he and this man had remained close.

"Anyway," Sean added, "Once I left their house, you were the first person I thought I should tell."

Charlie nodded. Naturally Sean had to tell *someone*. Charlie's own experience had been unusual, he suspected. He'd never had to "come out" per se, to his own family. It had always been just one more fact about him—handled with about the same amount of drama as his hair color or shoe size. His friends here in Boston had never been able to wrap their minds around it, especially once they discovered that he came from a pack of poncy British aristocrats.

But Charles never felt the need to apologize, because—welcome to the 21st century and all that, right?

"What did you say? Specifically, I mean?" Charlie tried again. If the man had wanted to talk, then Charlie had better get him talking. Sitting here grunting at each other was hardly going to accomplish anything.

Sean admitted, "For something I rehearsed so often, I actually don't remember. I know it was very formal and serious. Grim. Like someone had died or announced they had cancer."

Charlie waited.

Eventually, Sean asked, "How did you do it?"

"It was a long time ago," Charlie shrugged, thinking. "I…I can't explain it. I just always knew, and I made sure they did, too. From a young age, you know? My dad, the first time he said something like *Someday, you'll meet a lovely girl and you'll want to*…whatever…I don't recall his advice, really, just the beastly way I felt when he said it. I never wanted to feel like *that* again, and certainly not for the next ten or twenty years, so I had to say *something* back."

"Or, you could suck it up and stay quiet like the rest of us," Sean sneered.

Charlie gave him a little half smile. That wasn't his way, and Sean knew it. "I said something to the effect of, *I rather fancy Prince Charming, anyway, Dad.*"

Sean's eyes were round with admiration. "What did he do?" he breathed.

Charlie laughed. "Nothing. Didn't even flinch. He just said *Advice still stands*, then ambled away like he does."

Sean sat there shaking his head. "And you don't remember what the advice was?"

"I don't know," Charlie scoffed. "Some rubbish about being nice or respectful, likely." He drained his beer bottle, then signaled for another. "I figured they would want me to be that way with anyone, so it wasn't like it only applied to ladies." Charlie had always been a practical sort of bloke, but Sean was gazing at him like he was some kind of guru perched on the top of a mountain.

"I'm glad you did it, Sean," he commented softly, even though he knew the man probably didn't want to belabor the issue. "It needs to be in the open, for all of your sakes."

Sean nodded, and then, with an almost physical effort to change the subject, he asked, "Hey, how's your brother doing?"

Charlie didn't need to guess which brother Sean meant. Sean had never had a lick in common with steadfast Edward or silent, burly George. But young Fred—well, he and Sean had bonded instantly over Legos and Star Wars, and it melted Charlie's heart every time he witnessed it.

"He's good. Just got accepted to Tufts for next fall," he reported.

"Lemme guess—engineering?" Sean smiled.

Charlie laughed. "Yeah, of *course.*"

Fred had followed a fairly predictable trajectory from wooden alphabet blocks, to Legos and Erector sets, to intricate computer-aided design programs. As if that wasn't cool enough, he'd remained as hilariously prickly and put-upon as ever. They were all crazy about the little bastard. Charlie supposed everyone was, once they got to know him.

Sean's eyes meandered over Charlie's face and Charlie shifted, turning away to set down his beer. From the moment Charlie had met him, Sean had always been far too perceptive. Charles had to be very, very careful around him if he wanted to keep his secrets. It could be tiring, but he tried not to let it get to him. What was the point?

"And everyone else is good?" Sean prompted. Charlie knew he was being a terrible conversationalist. But there was just something different and unsettling going on between them tonight. Maybe it was because they didn't often go out one on one. Usually, there was a whole raucous group of them. Safety in numbers, both physically and emotionally, Charlie supposed. Imagine having a best friend you only saw in groups—it took some managing, that was for certain.

"Yeah, they're doing well. George and Poppy's wedding is coming up. Dad's got a new gig at BU. You know. Ed and Meg will have their girls in a few more months."

"What are they going to name them? Do you know?" Sean asked.

"Maybe Evie, maybe Isla. Definitely Lily," Charlie told him.

Sean put down his glass and stared in disbelief.

"What?" Charlie asked, baffled.

"You're shitting me, right?" Sean asked, incredulous.

"No," Charlie frowned. "Why?"

Sean cracked up—a manic, unsteady sound. "Seriously? You have to ask? What in the actual fuck, Charlie?"

Charlie just shook his head, not understanding. Had he lost his marbles?

Sean walked him through it. "Your mother is named *Violet*. George's fiancée is named *Poppy*. And now Edward is naming one of his daughters *Lily*? Good God, Charles, if you ever have a daughter, you're going to have to name her *Daffodil* or some shit."

Charlie snorted. "Hmm. Could hold up the adoption process—child cruelty and so forth. What about...*Gladiola*?" he chuckled.

"Christ, I think my grandmother grows those," Sean grinned.

Charles smiled merrily back. "Mine definitely does. That's the only reason I know what they are."

They fell back into a heavy silence, until Sean cleared his throat and asked, "And my girl, the countess?"

"Would probably tell you that you need to shave," Charlie laughed. "What's with the scruff?" He gestured to the two-day beard shadowing Sean's handsome face. His hair was a muddy light brown, but the hair on his face had a definite tinge of ginger to it. Charlie wondered how it would feel under his palm. Soft, or prickly? Likely exactly as his own did, he scoffed to himself. Why did he even bother? Thoughts like that would only get him in trouble.

"Oh, c'mon," Sean protested, shoving Charlie's arm. "Beards are totally a thing right now."

Charlie had to smile. Sean would stay on top of the trends until his last dying breath. But that was okay—nine times out of ten, they suited him perfectly.

"You seeing anyone these days?" Charlie blurted, wondering if maybe that explained the beard, or the new haircut. Or the way Sean seemed to be on edge, like he was feeling guilty for even being there.

Sean smiled, just a little. "No, not since that guy from Toronto. You?"

"No. I've been right busy, trying to finish things up in time for graduation."

Sean nodded. *Again.* God, when had things ever been so awkward between them? As much as Charlie would jump at any chance to be in the man's orbit, right now he was feeling pretty anxious to get away—if only to relieve the tense discomfort he was feeling.

Salvation came, in the form of a text from his brother:

Where the hell r u? Mum & Dad going home, ladies bunking down.

Bro Nite commencing in 30 mins

Charlie smiled. His brothers might be responsible sticks-in-the-mud these days, but they still wanted to celebrate Charlie's accomplishment. And he wasn't so spoiled that he couldn't feel grateful for that. Hell, they could even sneak Fred out, too—now that he was eighteen, that had gotten *quite* a bit easier than it used to be.

Charlie pushed to his feet, brandishing his phone. "Sorry mate, I gotta run. But hey—it was great seeing you."

"Yeah, you too," Sean said, looking serious as a heart attack. Charlie moved to go, but Sean stopped him with a hand on his arm. "Hey, Charlie?"

"Hmm?"

Sean glanced around quickly, confirming that they were still the only ones in the hotel bar. Even the bartender was gone, having headed into the back with a tray of dirty glasses several minutes ago. Next thing Charlie knew, he was pulled into Sean's embrace, surrounded by lean, strong arms in forest green cashmere, and Sean's spicy, woodsy cologne.

"Hey, Charlie," Sean whispered, mere centimeters from Charlie's mouth. And then, with an electric jolt to Charlie's system, Sean's mouth landed on his.

Chapter Two

SEAN HADN'T INTENDED to launch himself at Charlie, he truly hadn't. After he'd stepped out of his parents' row house, the one in which he and his two sisters had been raised, pretty much all he could think of was that he had to tell Charlie what he'd done. For six long years, Sean's life had been like that. Whether he aced a test or got a guy's number, it didn't seem real until Sean told Charlie Hughes and Charlie had weighed in on it.

And now, soaring free of the burden his sexual orientation had always been on the streets of Southie, where had Sean flown, but directly to his friend Charles. He'd completely forgotten what day it was, and Sean felt a qualm, certainly, that Charlie had deserted his beloved family on his graduation day to come meet him. Sean, moron that he was, hadn't even brought him a gift.

Seeing Charlie in person, now that Sean's big secret was no longer an issue, was harder than he'd expected. He was tongue-tied, watching the way the candle flickering on the table lit up Charlie's face. Watching the way his friend's brows came together in concern when Sean said what he'd come to say. Sean had been nursing the biggest crush this side of a Taylor Swift song for years on this guy.

Wicked bad—like, *incapacitating* bad. But cheerful, friendly, imperturbable Charlie had never once seemed to notice.

When he popped out of his chair and made to leave, Sean sort of panicked. He'd barely made the decision to declare himself on the cab ride over here—marrying actions to words seemed even farther out of the realm of reality.

And yet. He could now describe with total clarity what his "friend" kissed like. Tasted like. Felt like in his arms. And it was both exactly like he'd pictured—the flavor of Charlie's ever-present spearmint gum figured prominently—and nothing like Sean could ever have imagined. They were nearly the same height and had much the same lean, fit build. He wasn't sure, chest-to-chest as they were, whose freaking heart was pounding harder.

Sean supposed that sticking his tongue down the guy's throat might have communicated at least some of his message fairly well. But the finer points of his heart, the part where he'd never met a kinder, gentler, *wiser* human being than Charles Hughes—the part where Charlie was his best friend, where only Charlie's and his own sisters' opinions had ever mattered...well, Sean supposed he might need to scrounge up the actual words to express all that.

With a loud bang of the kitchen's door, the bartender backed into the room holding a tray of new glasses, and the two men sprang apart. Charlie stared at Sean, looking one hundred percent shell-shocked.

"I'm sorry," Sean began, holding out a shaking hand. "I didn't mean to —"

Charlie extracted his wallet from his jacket pocket and dropped some bills on the table. He glanced at the bartender, at Sean, at his feet. "I'm not sure this is the best place for this convo, mate," he murmured.

Right. Because going all soap opera on your homosexual crush, in the middle of a hotel bar, made perfect sense. God. Sean wanted to smack himself.

"Let me see if I can put them off," Charlie said, texting quickly. When the reply came in, he cursed. "No dice, mate," he told Sean, displaying the screen of his phone.

No can do, Guv. Cinderella needs to be home by 12 or he'll turn into a bloody pumpkin

"Okay, hey—don't worry about it," Sean rushed to assure him. "We can do this some other time."

"Fuck that," Charlie barked. "Just come with me."

"To see your brothers?" Sean squawked, getting more alarmed now.

"What? It's not like they bite," Charles scoffed.

"Are you sure about that?" Sean grumbled, remembering some of his friend's more lurid stories.

"Reasonably. At minimum, they wouldn't bite *you*." Then he paused. "You're not planning on provoking them, are you?"

"Um…no?" Sean offered.

"There. So you'll be fine," Charles blustered, then clapped his hands together like everything was settled.

THEY TOOK A cab over to yet another bar, this one a familiar pub the Hughes family seemed to favor. The other men were already there, gathered around a table at the back and eyeing Charlie and Sean's arrival with an unholy degree of interest.

Unfortunately, minutes after their arrival, Charles broke off from the group to hit the head. Which left Sean facing the inquisition all by himself. As a unit, the three remaining Hughes brothers turned on him with narrowed eyes.

"So…what are your intentions regarding our brother?" Fred finally inquired. Ah. So there would be no beating around the bush. It was just as well—Charlie couldn't possibly take that long in the men's room, could he?

Sean looked around the table. He could maybe take on Edward, though he thought Charlie might have mentioned at one point that this one was the boxer. One glance at George told Sean to not even *consider* crossing him. And it would be foolish to take a run at Fred— he was just young and stupid enough to be a danger to both himself and others. (Besides, he *liked* Freddy.) Sean might've been raised in Southie—and therefore had a healthy amount of scrap in him—but all three of these guys were a bit too much for him when he was this sober.

Which meant that Sean merely replied, "He's my best friend, man. I don't know what you mean." Fred, of all of them, ought to know that.

"Bullshit," George commented succinctly, though his lips twitched with humor. "You've been making cow eyes at him for years, mate."

Edward didn't say a word, just raised his eyebrows at Sean in an amused way that seemed to indicate *sell your crap to some other loser, asshole.*

Sean shrugged and tried again. "I just want him to be happy," he mumbled. Was no one going to offer him a fucking beer? Or better yet, something even stronger?

"Yeah, so do we," George growled. "Which is why we're wondering how many more years you plan on dicking around here. Are you *ever* going to make your move?" The smile he offered Sean was toothy and almost feral, but it seemed sincere enough. For a wolf.

"I...what?" Sean managed, squinting at him. It almost seemed like George *wanted* Sean to hit on his brother, but that couldn't be right, could it?

"It's become fairly obvious that you care about Charles quite a bit," Edward explained gently. Carefully, like he was leading Sean by the hand.

They all let that grenade settle, and waited for him to respond. So Sean admitted, "I do. A lot."

"It's become equally apparent to us how Charles feels about you," Ed continued smoothly. Like this was just your run-of-the-mill board meeting. His actual words took a moment longer to register than his tone. When they did...

Sean opened his mouth, but nothing in the way of actual words emerged. He didn't think *that* half of the equation was nearly so clear. He clamped his mouth shut again.

"Shut it," Fred hissed to his brother, like a B-movie villain. "Here he comes."

"Look, none of us are getting any younger here, okay mate?" George muttered under his breath. "You two are made for each other—just take the leap already," he urged.

"Also, our mum and dad really like you," Freddy added quickly.

"And us," Edward blurted. Fred and George nodded rapidly.

Charles strode up to the table and surveyed their faces. "Why does Sean look like he's about to puke?" he accused. "What did you wankers do to him?"

"Nothing!" Fred cried, with a hefty dose of teenage irritation.

George rolled his eyes. "Not a bloody thing, you paranoid arse."

Charlie then glared pointedly at Edward, clearly expecting him to be the voice of reason. Edward only smiled serenely. "Honestly, Charles, get a grip," he said. "Sean's fine. Aren't you, Sean?"

Sean licked his lips, but didn't trust his voice to come out normally. Instead, he gave Charlie a thumbs-up, picked up a mug that looked relatively untouched, then took a good long swallow of someone else's beer. If he wasn't mistaken, the Hughes brothers had just staged an intervention and urged him to make a move on their own brother.

GEORGE STOOD UP once the bartender brought over a new round of beers. Sean had the abrupt, uncomfortable sensation that he was crashing a private family gathering where he didn't belong, and cursed Charlie for making him come here.

"A toast, to our brother Charles." George lifted his pint glass and cocked his head in Charlie's direction. "We always knew you could do it, even when you didn't know it yourself."

Edward rose from his seat, too, more leanly elegant next to his brawnier brother. Sean was almost warier of him—he surmised that Edward's vengeance, if he ever vowed it, would be downright Machiavellian. George's would be bloody, but at least it would be brief. The fact that Sean had even figured all that out ought to be concerning, but it *had* been six long years.

"Thank you for finally proving us correct," Ed joked. "Now go out there and be brilliant."

They both turned to Fred, to check if he had anything to add. The youngest of the Hughes brood popped up out of his seat like a prairie dog, but clearly had not prepared his thoughts ahead of time. Of course he hadn't—you never knew what the hell was going to come out of the kid's mouth, and *usually* that was pretty entertaining. At eighteen, Freddy looked poised to be the tallest of all the brothers, and he was sweet, too. Hopefully he'd outgrow his inclination to try to keep up with his older siblings' witticisms, though. He raised his glass of soda high, paused for inspiration, then smirked.

"For he's a jolly good fellow," Fred intoned, then stopped, fresh out of ideas.

"That's it?" George bellowed.

"Which nobody can deny," Sean murmured, catching his friend's eye. Since he'd remained sitting, Sean was able to clink glasses with Charlie first. The others promptly sat and did so, too, with a hearty chorus of *hear-hears*.

What followed was about an hour of brotherly bantering, notable—to Sean, at least—for being both less respectful and more ribald than anything he'd ever uttered to his own two sisters. It was a shame that the oldest Hughes boys were already taken, he mused. Mary Kate, especially, would probably love them. Well, *secretly* love them, while outwardly spouting some jacked-up crap about the English and the Irish despising each other. Inside, Sean knew she'd work herself into a whole *West Side Story* passion. He'd seen it many times before, all through their childhood.

He couldn't rip on her too much, though, since Sean was secretly in love with the third Hughes brother. Must be some kind of Callaghan superpower, something in the genes—a certain dour repression that all in the family tree could be proud of. He sighed to himself. He had to be different. He couldn't keep living his life like that, not anymore. Sean was a grownup, he was out now, and he was in love with an amazing human being. He just had one more hurdle to get over, one last thing standing between him and happiness. He had to *tell* him.

FINALLY, GEORGE AND Edward, as if by some prearrangement, pushed to their feet.

"What, already?" Freddy cried, incensed.

"It's nearly eleven, Fred," Ed told him calmly.

"But Mum said I didn't have to be home until midnight! I have another whole hour, still!"

"No, you don't," George threatened, scowling at him.

Fred turned desperately to Charles for help, but Charlie just shrugged good-naturedly, thank God. "We'd hate for you to turn into a pumpkin in front of all these nice people," he smiled.

Sean looked around. The bar remained almost totally devoid of patrons, as it had been all along. Tomorrow night, with the families returning home and the graduation festivities over with, it would be a mob scene again.

"Come on, then," Charlie said to Fred, hauling him to his feet. "Walk with me a minute." They headed toward the street, while the rest of them dug bills out of their wallets to pay the tab.

Edward caught Sean's eye, his expression soft and encouraging. "So…your intentions?" he inquired again.

Sean saw that he wasn't going to be let off the hook, not tonight. So he went with stark honesty: "Honorable," he told them.

George snorted in disdain. "Honorable? That's the best you can do?" When that earned him an elbow in the ribs from Ed, he frowned, disgruntled.

Sean was fed up with this shit. Couldn't they give him a freaking chance to work stuff out before climbing all over him? He turned on George and belted out, "As honorable as they come, how about that motherfucker?" He clenched his fists, though he didn't want to have to use them. And he realized that he was maybe feeling a tiny bit testy, from the nerves no doubt, but still.

Edward nodded calmly, though, seeming satisfied by Sean's burst of temper. "Have at it, then," he said, magnanimous as fuck, suddenly. Like he'd needed some sign that Sean was serious, or something.

Charlie walked back to them, right as George cautioned, "Just don't cock it up, mate." Instead of answering, Sean watched Fred across the bar, forlornly throwing darts at a board mounted near the front door of the pub. He refused to promise something he wasn't sure he could deliver on, not even if George the Neanderthal knocked his teeth clear out of his skull.

Charlie called cheerfully, "What are we cocking up?" He turned to George. "You do realize that Sean and I are gay, right Georgie? *Cocking it up* is kind of what we *do.*"

"Oh, my God," Sean snorted, feeling his face flush red. Charlie was the worst. The best, in most ways, but also absolutely the *worst.*

Charlie turned to him, laughing. "Right?" he asked. He looked around, outraged that his joke had fallen flat. "Oh, come on, don't be a bunch of babies."

They heard a loud thunk and a curse, and swiveled to check on Fred. He had somehow managed to sink a dart in the side of the scoreboard, then, when he tried to remove it, apparently sent the whole thing crashing to the ground.

"Oh, here we go," George groaned, heading over to help. Edward waved off the bartender and moved to join them.

Sean knew he might not get another chance tonight. So he wrapped his hand around Charlie's arm and pulled him back. "We need to talk, man," he said.

"I know," Charlie agreed, more serious now.

"I'm pretty barred out," Sean admitted. "Why don't we grab a cab and head back to my place?"

It was a risk. Charlie could easily balk and go running back to his safe, loving family. And then Sean would probably sit on his sofa like a punk for the rest of the night, contemplating his miserable, lonely, Charlie-less existence.

But luck was apparently on Sean's side this evening, because Charlie nodded. "Let me get rid of these barmy blokes first, all right?"

"After you," Sean gestured grandly, waving at the two men doing a piss-poor job of hanging the dart scoreboard back on the wall, and the third fidgeting and looking guilty beside them.

Charlie sighed heavily, then squared his shoulders and stomped over. Sean shook himself. Now that he apparently had the go-ahead from the family, and was going to have his friend alone, what in the world was he going to say?

Chapter Three

CHARLIE STOOD IN the center of Sean's condo and tried to process what he was seeing. It was a big space and looked almost like a loft. Two-story ceilings, stark white walls, and a whole wall of slanting floor-to-ceiling windows framed in chrome. The furnishings were straight men's club, though: crimson oriental carpets and dark-brown leather Chesterfield sofas. Marble counters lined the open kitchen and mahogany end tables held neat stacks of magazines.

Sure, Sean had worked like a dog all through school, and had joined a prominent advertising firm directly upon graduating, but this was...

"Are you dealing drugs?" Charlie inquired.

Sean laughed, some of the tension broken. "God, you are such a prick. No, I'm not dealing drugs. My parents saved up for eighteen years to send me to college. When I won the Holton scholarship, I didn't end up needing their money. So, instead, they helped buy me a condo for graduation."

Charlie had met Sean's parents—they were not what anyone would call high rollers. He thought the father might even work for the sanitation department or something.

Charlie's thoughts must have shown on his face, because Sean added, "Preconstruction rates, you loser. It was a total steal." Sean beamed at that, pleased as punch. Charlie smiled back, amused as ever when his friend's accent slipped and he began dropping his r's. "Loser" had somehow become "loo-sah", and hell if the new version didn't convey disdain *very* effectively.

Charlie watched Sean for a minute, then walked over to check out the view. Straight-up Boston harbor. Lights twinkling on the water—probably moon and stars if the sky were clear. He turned back to his friend, wondering why he was here now, and why he hadn't been here *before* now.

"It's a three-bedroom," Sean commented, fussing with some bottles lined up perfectly by size on a gilt bar cart near the kitchen island.

"Are you plastered?" Charlie asked him, frowning. There had to be a reason this was happening, and it definitely had nothing to do with the number of Sean's bedrooms.

"Am I...what?" Sean stuttered, perplexed.

"I've never seen you drink more than one beer in the whole time I've known you. You drank three or four tonight," Charlie accused. "Some of them were even yours."

Sean shook his head in consternation. "*No.* No, Charles, I am not drunk. In fact, suddenly I feel about as sober as a Puritan preacher." *So*-bah. *Pree*-chah. Lord help him, Sean was doing it on almost every word. Was he nervous? What did he expect was going to happen here?

"Hell, if you can spit that out, you *must* be sober," Charlie claimed. This was probably not going the way Sean had envisioned, but how was that Charlie's fault? He wasn't the one blindsiding his friend for some unknown reason. "So...what are you getting at?" he blustered then, freaked out by this whole night, but determined to brazen it out as he always did. "You in the market for a flatmate or something?"

Sean shrugged a little, looking awkward. "Sort of," he murmured, studying the booze intently. "Eventually."

Charlie thought about that kiss in the hotel bar, and the way his brothers had been ribbing Sean, when they thought Charlie wasn't looking. "Or is it a flatmate with some fringe benefits that you're after?" he tried to joke, except this had stopped feeling funny roughly an hour or two ago, and he couldn't cough up a laugh.

Sean managed a smile, though. A sickly one, but it counted. "You're getting warmer," he said. Another dropped R. The man must be a wreck—or lying about being drunk.

Charlie opened his mouth to speak, but he really had no idea what he intended to say. Luckily, Sean forestalled him with a placating hand.

"Look, now that you're done with school, you're not going to want to stay with your parents forever. If you wanted, you could move in here until you get on your feet. Until you figure out what you want to do next," Sean explained, trying to sound reasonable and reassuring. "Find a job and whatnot."

"I see," Charlie snapped. He felt out of his depth, and he despised that feeling. "And what happens then?"

"We can renegotiate," Sean answered. Like this was all simple and normal and not remotely life-changing.

"Remove the benefits, you mean," Charlie groused, irritated. At what, he wasn't sure. He could say this, though: if Sean was hoping to start some temporary fling with him, he was not even kind of on board, no matter how well he kissed. Getting loved and then *left* by the man in front of him would destroy Charlie.

"Well, I was thinking more along the lines of adding in a license and two gold bands someday, but you know—you're the boss," his friend replied steadily. "That part doesn't have to happen right away, though. Obviously." Charlie wasn't positive, but Sean might have just alphabetized his liquor supply while sort of proposing—the bottles were no longer in height order, but still seemed to hold an inordinate amount of fascination for the other man. Charlie decided, given Sean's even delivery of bombshell after bombshell, that he probably ought to avoid playing poker with the man in the future. He was certain to lose big.

"My *father* wears a gold band," Charlie retorted. It was a reflex, and he sounded a bit like Freddy. Petulant. Affronted. Adolescent. It was the best he could manage at the moment.

"Forgive me," Sean huffed. "I'll be the stodgy one with the gold ring. You go ahead and wear something titanium with hideous black pinstripes if you want to."

Charlie stood there like a stone monolith, blinking at his friend. *Former* friend? *Christ.* Eventually, he managed to utter, "So it's like that, then?"

Sean visibly swallowed, stood up straight, and seemed to force himself to meet Charlie's provoking gaze. "It is exactly like that," he replied, brave and handsome as can be.

SEAN HAD *TRIED* to explain himself, though God only knew how well he'd done. He'd been so focused on moving his bottles of booze around the bar cart, like pieces on a goddamn chess board, because he was desperate to hide how badly his hands were trembling. What kind of man did this? Dropped a bomb on someone whose whole life was in transition? Or better yet, declared himself to his best friend, when he wasn't even *kind* of confident what the response would be? He'd—he'd maybe even just *save-the-dated* the man, in a roundabout, haphazard kind of way, despite having just kissed him for the first time hours before.

Sean felt faintly queasy, the three panicked mugs of beer he'd drunk swirling through his empty stomach like an angry winter sea.

To be fair, it was probably best he hadn't tried to down any supper—at this rate he'd be barfing on his buddy's shoes, along with hacking up professions of adoration. A real class act. Charlie didn't stand a chance.

In the cab, on the way back to his place, Sean had hesitantly taken Charlie's hand, lying there on the cracked pleather upholstery between them. Charlie went stiff beside him, but then, miraculously, his hand had moved, turning over to clasp Sean's. It was a little thing, certainly smaller than the man's response to his kiss, but that one modest gesture had given him the courage he needed to finally spill his guts to Charlie.

He should have anticipated that Charles would be a contrary asshole about the whole thing—it was his most frequently used defense mechanism. If Sean had planned for that, done his boy scout routine and been prepared instead of bumbling through this like a moron, maybe this night would be going better. Unfortunately, he suspected that if he'd given himself time to think, he would've chickened out. Now, however, Sean had to say *something* to fix this mess.

"Charlie —" he began.

Charlie cut him off, blunt as ever. "I'm in love with you, you know," he blurted, seeming to surprise even himself with the admission. "I've been in love with you since the moment you lent me a bloody pink highlighter sophomore year in typography class."

"Then why?" Sean wondered, too stunned to feel elation at the admission. "Why the five-year parade of Charlie's Angels, when you could have just told me?"

Charlie busted a gut at that. "Seriously? That's what you called them?" he laughed.

"Maybe," Sean muttered, feeling sullen. Five years of Charlie going on endless dates with ridiculous, stupid men. It had been torture to Sean's desperate, aching heart.

"Because I was an idiot. Because I thought I had to be sophisticated. Let me assure you, falling arse-over-elbow for the love of my life at a whopping nineteen years of age seemed like a move right out of the fucking rookie playbook. And also because…"

"What?" Sean demanded, when Charlie trailed off.

"Because I wasn't sure you'd actually made your peace with being gay," Charles admitted softly.

"Jesus, Mary, and Joseph, Charles! How can you say that to me?" Sean yelled, hurt and ashamed, all at once. "You know what it was like for me!" He was supposed to be Irish *Catholic*. How could Charlie not understand that?

"No, Sean, really. With everything I had going on, I couldn't exactly prop someone else up, too," Charlie insisted, gaze trained on his face.

Sean forced himself to calm down, knowing the truth of that. Making himself accept it.

"Things are different now," he explained, gripping the edge of the bar cart.

"It certainly seems that way," Charlie rejoined tartly.

Sean searched for a way to make him understand. He'd kissed the man, and Charlie had just punched him in the gut by telling Sean he'd been in love with him for years. So why did this still seem incomplete? Unresolved?

"Why now, Sean?" Charlie wanted to know. It was a valid question, and one that Sean at least *thought* he had an answer for.

"Well—I was out in Newton last week for a meeting. So I stopped by the Thompsons to say hello." Edward had introduced Charlie to the Thompson family a few years back, when he and George had done a renovation of their farmhouse. Within months of getting to know them, Charlie had brought Sean out to meet them, too. They were easy to love, that was for sure. And last week,

Sean had met their new baby, just adopted out of foster care like the others, and bringing the kid count up to four. It had blown his mind.

"Oh, yeah?" Charlie asked. "How are they?"

"Great. Happy. They brought home another baby," Sean told him.

"Really? That's brilliant. What do the other kids think?"

"They're over the moon. So are the guys—Mark quit his job, fired the nanny, and is staying home with them now."

"And Michael's okay with that?"

"No. He's totally envious. But you know them. They'll figure it out."

Charlie nodded, and kept nodding, longer than was necessary.

"So...what does that have to do with us?" he finally inquired.

Sean hesitated. "Well, you know how happy they all are."

"I do, yes." *Thank you, Captain Obvious, I can keep up just fine*, his tone said.

"I guess I just thought—why them, and not me? Why can't I have that, too? Because the only thing standing in my way all this time was apparently..."

"...you," Charlie finished for him.

"Me," Sean agreed, wincing. "And if I'm allowed to have a life like that, if I even *deserve* a life like that, then the only person I want that life with is you."

"I told you I love you. You do realize that, right?" Charlie inquired.

"Um, yeah," Sean admitted.

"Were you planning on returning the favor?" he asked.

"I might," Sean said, finally finding his balls and moving closer to Charlie. Charles took the last few steps himself, closing the distance between them, and slipping his arms loosely around Sean's waist.

"Now is good," Charlie murmured.

Sean smiled. Charles, bless him, had never been what one might call patient. "I love you," Sean told him. "I always have and I always will."

Charlie blinked at him fondly. Both of them were getting a little misty-eyed, though they'd go to their graves before either would admit it. To spare them from having to, Sean did the only thing he could think of to close the deal. He kissed him. Charlie kissed him back, a forever, pact-sealing kiss that took Sean's breath away.

God, he'd been lucky, in so many things. In that moment Sean knew, though, that he was luckiest in love.

Review

Did you enjoy **Lost in Love**? If so, please consider leaving a review at the retailer where you purchased this title.

Book reviews can be as simple or as detailed as you wish, but all of them help authors sell more books, and assist other readers in finding the stories they want to read.

Almost any book can be reviewed by simply logging into the website where you purchased the title, then scrolling to the bottom of the title's product page to find an area called "Leave a Review."

Up Next

Finding a Husband (*Lost & Found, Book 3*)

Everyone has secrets, but theirs could tear them apart.

Molly has learned the hard way that she does *not* need a man. What she does need is a job, and she knows exactly which one she wants. There's a law firm hiring down in North Carolina, and Molly knows she can't go wrong with the reliable paycheck, warm weather, and pristine beaches. Her brother-in-law has even hooked her up with a tour guide in town. It seems perfect—until that guide turns out to be the gorgeous, intriguing son of one of the law partners, and Molly has to concede that she's in way over her head.

Though Jake is just as wrapped up in her as she is in him, he's also holding something back. Their feelings for each other are undeniable. But when the secrets they're keeping threaten not only Molly's chance to land her dream job, but Jake's entire future, the couple must make some hard decisions—and soon. If they don't, their relationship and their hearts might never recover.

Can Molly and Jake overcome the crucial things they've left unsaid? Or will history repeat itself, and force them into lives they can't endure?

Finding a Husband

Chapter One

MOLLY RAISED HER tray table to its full upright position, then turned to peer down the aisle toward the back of the plane. As she did so, she was careful not to make eye contact with the man across the aisle from her, who'd been driving hard to the hoop pretty much since takeoff. The grim middle-aged woman on her other side had been no help at all—she'd popped a couple motion sickness pills before they even left the ground, and two hours later was still slumped boneless against the shaded window.

Molly had already run through most of her in-flight avoidance repertoire: feigning sleep, then intense interest in the programs on the airplane headphones—but now she had to use the bathroom. There was only about twenty minutes left before they began their descent into Wilmington, so she was going to have to play it exactly right. If she went too soon and the bathrooms were full, "Joe Friendly" over in 14A was only going to follow her back and try to flirt some more. If Molly waited too long, she'd miss her chance— and no one wanted that. It was probably too late to pretend she didn't speak English, given that he'd heard her talking to the flight attendant for the last three hours or so.

Molly checked again and saw a balding, paunchy businessman exit the bathroom on the right. Okay, there was her cue. She flicked open her seatbelt and stood, using the empty headrests for balance as she made her way to the back of the plane. Halfway there, a kid spilled into the aisle in front of her, glasses askew and socks falling off his feet. With jerky, loping steps, he bee-lined for the open bathroom, and locked himself inside. *Damn.*

Molly didn't want to go back and start all over again. Instead, she passed through the short hallway with its two occupied lavatories, then searched the small kitchen area beyond for a flight attendant. If she could strike up a conversation quickly, she might be able to ignore Joe Friendly if he came hunting for her. Molly snorted. *If* was wishful thinking—knowing Joe, he was probably already on his way.

A touch on her arm confirmed her fear. "Hey there," he said. "I think you dropped this!" Molly turned around, frowning. Joe extended a small paperback of Sudoku puzzles toward her.

"Oh, sorry. That's not mine," she told him. She tried to be polite, but this had gotten ridiculous roughly fifteen minutes into the flight. Joe couldn't seem to take a hint and it was wearing thin.

"You sure? I could swear it fell right off your lap when you got up," he insisted.

"Nope. Never seen it before in my life." Molly gave him a vague, noncommittal sort of smile, then let her eyes slide away.

"Huh, that's weird," Joe mused, leaning on the wall across from her and giving Molly an obvious once-over.

The flight attendant in the kitchen finished arranging things in his cabinet and turned to them. Molly sighed, and deflated a bit more. Of *course* it would be the only male attendant on the flight, who seemed to view himself as some kind of high-altitude Casanova.

"I can take that for you," he said briskly. He whisked the little book out of Joe's hands and tossed it in a trash bag hanging from a cart, then shot Molly a conspiratorial smile. Now that he was facing her directly and not looming over her shoulder, she could see that his name tag read "Chad." Molly had already noticed his fake tan and blindingly white teeth—it was the stubble growing between his thick black eyebrows that was the real surprise. *Huh*. Chad apparently waxed his brows—but not often enough, it seemed. That was something new.

Molly kept her pleasant expression pasted on her face, but turned slightly away from them, letting her eyes go unfocused again as she stared off into the distance. Usually that worked quite well to communicate the *not-interested* vibe, but these two were hard cases.

Joe nudged her again. "Get a load of that," he snorted, tilting his head toward the bathroom the kid was locked inside. Horrible heaving noises could be heard within, and Molly grimaced, hoping the other door was the one that opened first.

Chad tossed his head and pushed himself officiously between them. "I'll take care of it," he said, rapping on the door. "Everything okay in there?" he called more loudly.

The kid fell silent, and the water turned on. "I'm okay," the little guy whimpered.

Chad rolled his eyes and smiled at Molly again. "We'll give him another minute or two. If he doesn't come out, I'll walk you up to first class, okay?"

Because...she couldn't find her way up to first class all by herself, Molly thought drily. There was that short, totally straight aisle to navigate, after all—and the daunting blue curtains, closed at the end. She didn't respond like she wanted to, though. She'd learned the hard way that people didn't react well to an attractive woman with a bad attitude.

So, Molly simply rubbed a hand over her face and muttered, "Thanks."

Joe didn't appreciate getting knocked out of position by the other man. He lifted his chin at Chad and blustered, "Hey, guy. You got any beer back here?"

Chad was not in the mood to hydrate the competition, though. He stared Joe down and snapped, "Sorry. We put everything away.

Drink service ended ten minutes ago." Molly had no doubt he'd find something for *her*, if she asked—but she wasn't going to hand that minor victory to him.

Joe nodded, looked around one more time—and then seemed to realize that Molly would have to return to her seat eventually. With one last smarmy look her way, he shuffled back up the aisle and collapsed into 14A to wait her out.

Chad elbowed her, a bit too hard. "He bothering you?"

"No, it's all good. Thanks, though," Molly sighed. She absolutely hated being a captive audience. Between the seat belt sign and the inconvenient fact that they were however-many feet up in the air, there was nowhere for her to *flee*.

"No problem," Chad said. "Do you live in Wilmington, or are you just visiting?"

"Oh. Um, just visiting." Molly stared desperately at the bathroom doors. What in God's name was taking these people so long?

"Got some family there?" Chad prodded, unwilling to cede the field when he was so obviously seducing her like a boss.

Molly did actually have family in the area, but admitting it seemed unnecessary. Instead, she droned, "No, I'm heading down for a job interview." Like it was the worst thing in the world, instead of the best.

When she made to look away, Chad ducked down a bit to maintain eye contact. "Yeah? What do you do?"

"I'm an attorney," Molly told him flatly. Chad apparently hadn't been expecting that, because he reared back and had nothing at all to say in response. Not *That's hot*. Not *What are you, some kind of nerd?* Nothing.

At last, the kid emerged from his bathroom, looking wan and shaky. Molly and Chad eyed him as he staggered back up the aisle, then both turned back to the open bathroom door. With a huge intake of air, Chad steeled himself to peek inside—and was already shaking his head when he pulled out again.

"Don't go in there if you can help it," he told her with a wince. He reached into a cabinet for some paper towels and a bright green spray bottle, clearly hating life in that moment. Even Chad was going to have problems making disinfectant look sexy.

Molly blew out her own breath and stared at the other door hopefully. Maybe that person was only changing their clothes, or putting on makeup, or shaving. Something benign, sweet-smelling, and noncommunicable.

"So…" Chad began, setting the green bottle back down again. Molly could tell what was coming by his tone alone. "Why don't I give you my number? We can get together while we're both in town."

Molly shrugged, and held up her empty hands. "Left my phone in the seat pocket." Not that she expected it to work, but it was still worth a try.

Chad scowled at her. "You shouldn't do that," he scolded. "It could get stolen."

"Good to know," Molly retorted. Her phone was jammed in the back pocket of her jeans, pressed safely against the wall behind her. Did he think she was stupid?

"No joke," Chad emphasized. "But here —" He took his own phone out of his pocket, and said, "Give me your number, and I'll hit you up for drinks later."

Molly knew it was pointless—she didn't even bother resisting. She recognized, from long experience, that fighting simply took too much time and energy. Instead she said, "Sure. It's 617…" Molly rattled off the digits she knew by heart, and didn't even feel guilty about it.

The other door opened then, and Molly didn't wait. She spun and ducked in with one smooth motion, then slid the lock home behind her. The atmosphere inside, *naturally*, was a fetid miasma that choked her on her first inhale. Eyes watering, Molly tucked half her face inside her shirt collar, slapped her phone on the sink counter, and wrenched her jeans down. She'd better take care of business as soon as possible or she was liable to suffocate in there.

It seemed that Chad was content to get back to work, now that he had Molly's number in his possession. When she emerged from the bathroom—gasping for fresh air—he'd already left for the front of the aircraft. Molly could see him bending over the first-class passengers, his oily smirk firmly affixed to his face. She still had to contend with Joe in the seat across from her, though—as the plane began its landing sequence, he leaned into the aisle with his best winning pitch.

"I'm only in town for a couple days," he told Molly. "But hey— why don't we grab some dinner later? I know a great place right on the river. They make a mean margarita."

"Sorry, I can't," Molly replied. "I've got a meeting later." It was a date with room service, but how would he know?

"That's all right," Joe assured her. "I can wait. Here's my number. Call me when you're done, and we'll meet for drinks." He handed her his business card—Joe Friendly, it seemed, was actually named "Mike," and worked in software sales.

"Not sure if I can swing that, but thanks," Molly told him. He was watching what she did with the card, so instead of cramming it into the ashtray in her armrest, Molly tucked it into the outer pocket of her leather tote—soon to be joined by her used boarding pass and all the other travel ephemera she planned to throw away later.

"Why don't you give me your number, too?" Joe/Mike said. "You know, to be safe?"

Molly groaned under her breath, then rattled off those ten sweet digits she knew so well. They rolled right off her tongue—like a lullaby, or a prayer. She only hoped that Chad and Mike liked their fast-food burritos delivered.

THE PLANE WOULD probably be on the ground in ten minutes, but Molly retrieved her laptop from her bag anyway. Once she started it up, though, she simply sat there staring blankly at the screen, deep in thought. Her connections—such as they were— appeared to be paying off. When Molly told her sister about this trip, Mina had immediately drafted her husband, Grey, to help.

He had an interesting history, but it was a useful one. After spending three years in the service, Grey took a break from the military to attend college. He'd gone to UNC Chapel Hill, where he'd been the president of the DKE fraternity—despite being both older and a married man at the time. After graduation, Mina's husband rejoined the Marines as an officer, and he remained one to this day.

As it turned out, Grey had a fraternity brother who, conveniently, lived in Wilmington. "Jake" had agreed to look out for Molly while she was in town, after little more than a casual phone call from her brother-in-law. She wasn't entirely sure what that entailed—yet more "drinks" would probably be involved. But given the fact that Molly had rarely known a soul in any position to help her, she was inclined to accept the favor with a grateful heart. Even if Grey could be a bit odd, and any friend of his was probably suspect, too. Though Jake had seemed normal enough when he'd texted to arrange things, Molly knew she should be careful.

At the very least, Molly was looking forward to some warmer southern weather. Winter had been extra cold in Boston this year, and it had been difficult not to get taken in by the fishing photos her dad sometimes emailed her. Out of the two vastly-different locales her parents had landed in, Molly had fallen hard for her father's current home. And no wonder—those beautiful Carolina beaches were real heartbreakers. Knowing she could live there full-time—if she played her cards right—had made the long, gray winter and abrupt populace of Molly's current town much harder to stomach lately.

Molly had to get her ducks in a row, regardless. First off, she had to land a real job soon, since her part-time gig at the legal aid office wasn't going to hold her for much longer. Molly had student loans from two degrees coming due, now that she'd graduated. She also lived in a sublet room in a group house—whose lease, she'd recently learned, was nearing its end.

Her family, God knew, would be no help whatsoever. Somehow, despite all her careful planning, Molly had ended up in a fix. She needed to find something fast and didn't want to make a rash decision because of it.

In the current hiring climate, Molly would have to make her own luck. She needed to be savvy and clever to land the perfect job. The alumni office at school hadn't come up with many leads, so she'd worked the internet, done her research, and lined up a few interviews for herself.

There was only one position Molly really wanted, however, and that was the junior associate job at *Alexander, Polk & Futch*, in Wilmington, North Carolina. They had taken the unusual step of flying her down and putting her up in a bed and breakfast for two weeks—so she could get to know the firm and attorneys, and submit to a round of interviews to see if she was "a good fit." Molly intended to be more than good—she was aiming to be *perfect*.

It didn't help her frame of mind—her necessary *focus*—that her life had gotten weirdly isolated and lonely for someone so used to being in demand. The people she knew in Boston were beginning to move on from this stage in their lives. Leaving town, getting jobs, getting married. Her best friend and roommate from undergraduate school, Meg, was the most glaring case. Molly could only talk about true love so often with her before turning a little green—because Molly knew how fickle and false the emotion could be. True, Meg's fiancé Edward seemed devoted enough, but…you never could tell, could you? Molly knew that for a fact.

She'd keep an eye on Meg. And Molly herself would stick with what had worked for her all this time—when you were pretty and popular, people didn't tend to cross-examine you about your private life. And when you were smart on top of that, good things came your way. Which was fine, because Molly's plans for herself did *not* include following in her parent's footsteps—the less she was judged for their choices, the better.

She wasn't going to be shiftless and disloyal like her father. And she wasn't going to marry for looks or money like her mother. Molly's prime directive for years had involved working hard and avoiding anything or anyone that reminded her of her mom, dad, or a certain young man named Carter. It worked like a charm, too.

Molly shook herself back to the present, glanced across the aisle at Mike, then opened her browser and called up her bookmarked list of favorite websites. In seconds, she was staring at a large photo of a beautiful Victorian house right in the middle of historic Wilmington. It was a confection, really—pastel yellow with gingerbread trim, colorful pots of flowers hanging from the porch ceiling, and dark green shutters. It was exactly the kind of house Molly had always dreamed of living in—someplace she could stay long enough to know the neighbors, and even the neighbors' kids and dogs.

She sighed, eyeing the estimated value of the property. On the one hand, it didn't seem terribly expensive compared to houses in the suburbs of Boston, or even the new condos downtown. But on the other hand, Molly didn't know how much the salary of a bottom-rung attorney would stretch down there. Soon, though, she would know if her life was taking a turn for the better. Soon, she'd know if she could afford a real home like the one in the picture. Molly nodded. One step at a time—she was so close now.

IN THE BAGGAGE claim, Molly found Grey's friend lounging against a wall and holding a hand-lettered sign with her name on it.

He was tall and broad-shouldered, with sandy-blond hair and sparkling blue eyes framed by inky lashes. As Molly assessed him, she noted that he was painfully clean-cut—his studied casualness both preppy and reeking of wealth. Molly felt her herself stiffen, already on guard for what was sure to be an arrogant opening statement.

Grey hadn't mentioned that Jake was a looker, but what could she expect? As oblivious as her brother-in-law was, he probably didn't even realize. If not that, he might have assumed Molly would be immune, as she usually was.

She smoothed back her ponytail and stood a little straighter, wishing she'd put on some lipstick in the airplane bathroom. She hadn't wanted to encourage either Chad or Mike, though. If Molly was using her head, she wouldn't want to encourage this guy, either. It was better to view things like clothes and makeup as armor—an essential barrier holding trolls like this one at arm's length, and *not* as invitations to get closer.

Jake might be gorgeous, but Molly knew better than most what could hide behind a handsome face. She wasn't fooled by his crooked, charming smile for one minute. She'd have to be just as wary of this frat brother from the Dekes as she would any other guy—probably even more so. A woman should never underestimate the rot that might harbor inside a shiny, rich shell, after all. Even if that shell was pushing off the wall and heading right toward her, grinning charmingly. Jake had clearly been supplied with a physical description of Molly, because he was suddenly a man on a mission.

"You must be Molly," he drawled when he reached her side. He was so certain of himself that he crumpled his little sign and dropped it right in a trash can on his way.

"Yup," Molly agreed. She glanced around the area, wishing for a vending machine or a little kiosk where she could buy some water. The air wafting in from the sliding doors smelled of diesel fuel and cigarette smoke—and it was way hotter and more humid than Boston's.

He stuck out his hand. "I'm Jake." her tour guide looked a little taken aback by how terse Molly was. She didn't like being this unfriendly, but the truth was—she'd been surprised by the way Jake's looks affected her. It had thrown her off-balance, and she was scrambling to find her footing.

"Nice to meet you," Molly told him, though she kept her tone chilly. "I told Grey you didn't have to do this, but he kind of insisted." *Good. Now he wouldn't think this was her idea.*

"No worries. I didn't have a lot going on at work this week. I'm happy to show you around a bit." His voice was smooth and deep, with a touch of Southern twang. Molly hated to admit it, but it was a voice absolutely *made* for the bedroom.

She forced herself to look away from the sexy mouth uttering those words, away from Jake's open collar and tanned throat. She wouldn't be anywhere near a bedroom with this guy, because she had learned her lesson far too well the first time she'd met a man like him. Molly was no fool, and never, *ever* made the same mistake twice. Not now. Not ever.

In the knot of other passengers swarming the baggage claim, Molly noted both Chad and Mike hurrying by. Chad caught her eye and gave her a little salute that he probably thought looked spicy, but he didn't pause. Mike waited a moment or two to be sure he had her attention, then raised the slip of paper he'd written her number on in greeting. Had it ever left his hand? Molly wondered—for the umpteenth time in the last few years—if the men would even realize she'd given them the wrong number on purpose, or if they'd assume the mistake was accidental. She sighed heavily.

"What the heck was that all about?" Jake inquired. He strolled after her, then easily grabbed her bags off the carousal when she reached for them.

"They spent half the flight jockeying for position—I had to give them my number just to get rid of them," Molly explained, rolling her eyes. Jake probably thought she sounded like a snot, but she couldn't let herself care. It was probably a good lesson for him, anyway.

"Seriously?" he gaped, turning to check out the other men. "Not your real one, right?"

"Are you nuts? I've been handing out the digits for a 24-hour Taco Bell for six years now." Molly didn't usually like to let guys peek behind the curtain—especially ones she wasn't good friends with—but she was only here for two weeks. She'd be gone before much could come of it, and besides, what was Jake going to do? Rat her out to every guy she'd ever met in a bar?

Instead, he chuckled—a rumbling, erotic sound that warmed Molly's insides. She'd been trying to ignore his sultry voice, but he hadn't laughed like *that* yet. It was probably for the best that he'd kept it under wraps—Molly might have found an excuse not to meet him otherwise, out of sheer self-preservation.

He tried another smile on her. "So. How was your flight?"

"It was fine. Other than those two, obviously." She jerked a thumb at Mike, standing at the information counter. Chad had already jammed a cigarette between his lips and disappeared outside.

"This all you got?" Jake inquired. He hoisted her big bag up on his shoulder and adjusted his grip on her hanging bag. He was wearing a button-down shirt with the sleeves rolled up, a worn pair of khaki shorts, and boat shoes. Jake was fit and clean and tan, and might have been a model in some trendy, overpriced clothes catalog. Molly repressed a shudder. Jake was everything she tried to avoid if she could help it.

"Yeah," she told him. "That's it." Then she clapped her hands together, forced any thought of how good he smelled from her mind—was that his deodorant, or some insidious new kind of cologne?—and turned toward the sliding doors. "Where to?"

ALEXANDER, POLK & FUTCH was having Molly's rental car delivered to the B&B, but not until early the next morning. Until then, Molly was on her own, and she would have been fine hailing a cab—but Grey and Mina had been adamant.

They'd wanted her to meet up with this friend of theirs right from the get-go, and hadn't budged on the idea despite Molly's initial protests. When they told her Jake was a prosecutor in Brunswick County, Molly had supposed it couldn't hurt to get his take on the legal community there—so eventually she'd agreed. The more she'd thought about it, the more it made sense. But that was before she'd seen for herself what kind of guy Jake was. Now, she was here in Wilmington, at some frat boy's mercy.

Molly groaned to herself. Calling Grey a *complicated* guy was being generous, so having to be shepherded around by a man that had somehow earned her brother-in-law's seal of approval suddenly wasn't sitting all that well. What had she been thinking? Molly should've known better—she'd rubbed shoulders with her share of frat guys during college, and certainly her share of boys who were full of themselves. But when Mina and Grey arranged this whole thing with Jake, Molly was so staggered at the notion of Grey being helpful, that she hadn't really stopped to consider the ramifications of what she'd agreed to. She felt touchy and irritable about it now, and when Jake waltzed her up to his shiny new Audi out in the short-term lot, well…her bad mood took a bit of a nosedive.

Inside the hot car, Molly caught another whiff of Jake's cologne when he shifted to put on his seatbelt. She cringed. The scent was faint, but crisp and pleasant. If she'd been smelling it in the middle of a department store, for example, she might have even liked it. Ever since the debacle that was Carter, however, Molly had an aversion to men who wore cologne. For the most part, they seemed like preening, effeminate dandies. Except—that characterization might not apply here.

The man sitting beside her was both exactly like Carter…and *nothing* like him. The problematic cologne was light enough to possibly be his deodorant—it *was* really humid out—or maybe even his laundry detergent. Molly only caught a fleeting hint of it when the breeze changed direction or he moved a certain way. Whatever she was smelling, the urge to get closer, to get a nose full of it, was maddening.

By now, Carter might have even managed to tell her what scent he was wearing—and how much it cost. Molly, at age seventeen, would have been suitably impressed. In contrast, Jake looked completely oblivious to the whole entire *thing* going on in Molly's head.

She sat back in her seat and fought a shimmer of confusion, of *doubt*, that whispered down her spine. Damn it, she had her rules for a *reason*, and Molly would be a colossal idiot if she forgot them all now—her career and her future were on the line. No frat guys. No rich guys. No smug bastards, and *definitely* no men wearing cologne. She had never had occasion to question those dictates before now, and today should be no exception.

It would be okay, Molly told herself, trying to stay calm. Jake could drive her to her B&B, and thereby satisfy the agreement he had with Grey. Molly would then go about her business, interviewing at the firm—like a rock star—for the next two weeks like nothing had happened. If Jake tried to see her again, she would simply say she was too busy, and put him off. Easy. Grey and Mina would be content that they'd helped her in their own small way. Jake would be off the hook and could return to his regularly-scheduled life. And Molly would secure her dream job for herself without any good-looking, good-smelling interference.

It was an excellent plan, and it would have worked. It *should* have worked. But then, on the highway heading away from the airport, Jake started shooting her *significant* looks.

"What?" Molly demanded, frowning at him. For a guy getting the arctic treatment, he was awfully cheerful.

Jake smirked, "You think you've got me all figured out, don't ya darlin'?"

Molly pressed her lips together in annoyance, then blurted, "Look, Jake, I'm sure you're a very nice person, but I've met plenty of guys like you before. I've even dated some of them. So, yeah, I can say with confidence that I know exactly what your deal is." She shrugged dismissively. God, she sounded like a shrew, but it had to be done. Better that she not lead him on and give him any untenable ideas about her.

"Is that so?" Jake arched one quizzical brow at her, then looked back to the road. One casual hand was draped across the top of his steering wheel, and the other rested on his gearshift, disconcertingly close to her thigh.

"Mm-hm."

"Lemme guess—I'm a spoiled frat guy raising hell with Daddy's money, leaving a trail of roofies and broken hearts in my self-absorbed wake. That about cover it?"

Whoa. He was good. "Pretty much," Molly agreed, feeling defensive. But given how badly she'd just insulted him, she couldn't quite figure out what he found so entertaining.

"Well, I am also confident that I've got *your* number," Jake told her, glancing over at her again. Could eyes dance? Because his baby-blues appeared to be dancing. At minimum, they were annoyingly sparkly.

"*Please,*" Molly scoffed. "You don't know anything about me." She hoped.

"Oh, like you know *me* from Adam? How 'bout this? Everything comes easy for you and now you're frustrated because you can't find a single challenge worth sinking your teeth into. I bet you just flew through school, didn't you?" He paused to eye her, then nodded to himself, satisfied that he was on the right track. "You've been getting too much attention for all the wrong reasons, probably for years. So now, if a guy has the nerve to notice that you're a pretty girl, you write him off from the get-go—because no way in hell is he gonna respect you for your smarts, right? All men want to do is beg, borrow, and steal their way into your bed."

Molly sat there feeling slightly sick. Who the hell *was* this guy?

"Am I right, Miss Molly?" Jake asked again, not letting her off the hook.

She swallowed. "Maybe a tad," she admitted softly.

"Look. I'm not an asshole just because I know Grey, or because I was in a fraternity, or because my family has some money," Jake told her gently. "How about throwing me a bone, and not sentencing me before I've had a fair trial?"

Molly finally had to laugh—because *of course* another attorney would say that.

"All right," she said grudgingly. "I'm sorry I was being a bitch. Truce?"

"Truce," he smiled, and Molly looked away again, blinded by all those white teeth, those blue, blue eyes, that tan skin, and that sun-kissed hair. Geez, he looked like Barbie's boyfriend, "Southern Charm Ken." The more her mind chewed on his words, though, the more she zeroed in on one phrase in particular. It wasn't the one where he'd called her pretty. It *wasn't.*

"Why would I think you were an asshole because you know Grey?" she asked, squinting curiously at him.

"He's *your* brother-in law," Jake retorted, but when his gaze flicked to her, his eyes were wary. "You tell me."

God. *That* was a loaded question. Molly had never liked or trusted her sister's husband—but she'd been keeping that a closely-held secret for more than ten years. As far as she could tell, she was the only person on earth who didn't love the guy. Except, maybe, for this man, who had suddenly turned a lot more intriguing.

"Grey has his moments," she replied vaguely. She'd certainly thrown that comment out before—no reason it wouldn't work again.

Jake turned and raised both eyebrows at her, calling *bullshit*.

"Not all of them stellar," Molly admitted.

"Ya think?" Jake laughed again, but he didn't say more. That was probably for the best. Molly had been lying to her sister Mina for years about how she felt about Grey—it would get even harder to do if Molly was in possession of sordid college tales about him.

"Almost there," Jake murmured, cutting into her thoughts. "How about some lunch before I drop you off?"

"Sounds great," Molly replied absently. It wasn't what she'd intended to do, but absolutely none of her meeting with Jake was going as she expected. Later, she was going to have to process what that might mean.

To read more, please purchase **Finding a Husband** from your favorite bookseller!

FREE BOOK

Get a glimpse of Morgan, Meg, Molly and Mina—*before* their happily ever afters take place!

Sign up for the author's Reader's List and get a free copy of the Lost & Found prequel novella "Girls Night Out."

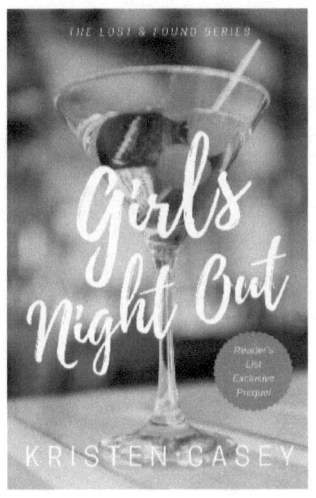

Visit Here to Get Started:

http://eepurl.com/ctGk1j

Also by Kristen Casey

The Triple Threat Series

The Titan Was Tall

The Doctor Was Dark

The Hero Was Handsome

The Masquerade was Magic

The Hero's Brother

The Triple Threat Box Set

The Black Watch Security Series

False Flag

Heat Seeking Missile

Brothers in Arms

Fight or Flight

Search and Destroy

Squared Away

Acknowledgements

An author never gets from point A to point B without a lot of help, and I am no exception. I'd like to thank my two editors and beta-readers, Helen and Miss Laura, for their herculean efforts. You'll probably never know how grateful and touched I am that you took time away from your families and busy schedules to read and edit my manuscript. But my book, my readers, and most of all *I* thank you. Your eagle eyes and insightful comments made this book so much better.

I am delighted, once again, to also thank Deborah at Tugboat Design for her beautiful book cover design. Her suggestions and insight remain the best in the business, and she's a genuinely nice person, to boot. Her work may happen "behind the scenes" of a book but trust me when I say—it's splendid.

Thanks go to my readers, too! You never miss an opportunity to tell me in person how much you've enjoyed my books. You write me the *best* reviews online. And sometimes, you even send your kids to school with messages for my kids about how much you loved my novel. That will never get old—so keep it up!

Last, no thank you would be complete without mention of my incredible family. My husband and children remain my most supportive, caring, fanatical fans—and that is a gift I will forever be grateful for. Thanks for that, and for making your own meals when Mom is tucked behind her computer screen and acting a bit…touchy. You are truly the cats' pajamas.

About the Author

Kristen Casey writes the kind of heartfelt, steamy books she loves to read—full of relatable characters and delicious dialogue. She lives in Maryland with her husband, kids, and assorted cats, and in her free time, she enjoys all things crafty—especially projects she finds on Pinterest.

Sign up for her newsletter to receive exclusive free content and the inside scoop on sales and new releases—all emailed right to your inbox.

You can also follow her on social media for behind-the-scenes tales, character and setting inspiration, book reviews, and more:

Goodreads: Kristen_Casey
Facebook: AuthorKCasey
Twitter: AuthorKCasey
Pinterest: KristenCase0461
Instagram: Kristen.Casey.Books
BookBub: Kristen Casey
TikTok: KristenWritesRomance

Reading Order of Kristen's Books

The Lost & Found Series

Girls Night Out (Prequel exclusive to subscribers)

Finding Home (Book 1)

Finding Love (Book 2)

Lost in Love (Book 2.5—Includes *Lucky in Love*)

The Flynn Sisters Box Set (Includes *Christmas in Cambridge*)

Finding a Husband (Book 3)

Finding Forever (Book 4)

Forever and a Day (Book 4.5—Includes *Forever Starts Now*)

The O'Connell Sisters Box Set (Includes *Heroes & Husbands*)

The Triple Threat Series

The Titan was Tall (Book 1)

The Doctor was Dark (Book 2)

The Hero was Handsome (Book 3)

The Triple Threat Box Set (Includes *The Masquerade was Magic* and *The Hero's Brother*)

The Black Watch Security Series